Hunt Me

Love Thieves Book 3

By

Heather Long

Published by Decadent Publishing Company, LLC
Look for us online at:
www.decadentpublishing.com

~A Note from the Author~

Dear Reader,

The search for *The Fortunate Buddha* began in *Catch Me* and continued in *Treasure Me* comes to a rollicking conclusion in *Hunt Me*. I have always loved a good mystery. Even more, I love action adventure. The best part of a romantic suspense is marrying the two together.

Kit and Jarod like Sophie and Pietr before them are one of my all time favorite couples. I've always found mental challenges to be even sexier than the physical, luckily in Hunt Me, I got to play with both. I hope you enjoy them as much as I did.

Heather

The value of the Fortunate Buddha *is not the precious stones or metals, but the legend of good luck it brought to the temple visitors who made a wish and a prayer while rubbing its ruby-studded belly.*

Three things cannot be long hidden: the sun, the moon, and the truth. – Buddha

Chapter One

arod Parker peeled back the layers of latex and faux skin disguising the shape of his jaw and neck. Next, he removed the addition to his cheeks and ducked his face into the water. In minutes, he washed away the Walter Curry appearance he manufactured when he dealt with his assets. Glancing at the mirror again, he studied his altogether nondescript face. A single scar ran parallel to the underside of his right eye. It wasn't discernible most of the time, unless someone looked closely. At thirty-five, he could make himself look anywhere from his early twenties to his late fifties.

His cropped close and typically dark hair appeared salt and pepper from dealing with the Kingston situation. A good shampoo would correct the lingering color. With precision, he stripped his button-down shirt and suit pants. He hung everything up, leaving it on the rack for the housekeeper to collect.

Fifteen minutes later, showered and shaved, he strolled through the three-level townhouse in search of the files he'd brought home. Rubbing the back of his neck, he carried his briefcase and its contents back to his bedroom and left the towel slung over a wooden chair back before sprawling on the bed. Phone in hand, he flipped open the information he'd collected.

Reports filed by Anya on her initial issues reclaiming the Buddha in Morocco—including the details about recruiting Max to put the item back. A second statement from Max detailing the theft of the item between the time he returned it to the vault and the meeting with the ambassador a few hours later. Jarod flipped open his phone and dialed a number for the asset he had on site in

Morocco.

"Renard, is he planning to attend the auction in Ankara?" If Walter's brisk manner and clipped tone surprised the man, he said nothing about it.

"No, sir. Not as I can tell. I think the Buddha incident has scared him off. He's limiting his art acquisitions to proper channels."

"Keep an eye on him."

"Yes, sir."

They rang off, no pleasantries, no catching up, and a call lasting less than thirty seconds much less likely to be traced. So the ambassador was out of the game. The next statements included police reports, text messages, and a handful of news stories from Geneva. No mention of the break-in at Louis duMonde's corporate building, but plenty of Max slugging the French viscount at the party.

The bagged note of apology to Anya yielded no fingerprints or DNA. It had been printed right there in the office, so no way to trace the computer back to the culprit and the single letter K as the signature.

He stood, stretching, and padded naked back down to the kitchen.

K.

He stared unseeingly at the coffee maker as he reviewed his mental notes from the file. Twice the Buddha had been removed in and around Anya's actions. She had it in her possession a brief time, they returned it, and it was stolen again.

Louis duMonde's involvement with the theft from the ambassador's mansion in Morocco fit the facts. The idea he must have used an accomplice also fit the facts. The coffee hissed into his cup, and the Keurig shut off. Cup in hand, he returned up the stairs. The facts also provided enough to detail to suggest another thief took it from duMonde in Geneva even as Max and Anya tried to reclaim the item.

The second individual clearly didn't work with duMonde.

In one corner, duMonde and his men, in another, the IAAR— International Art and Antiquities Recovery agency for which Walter ran an entire division of assets—and, in the third corner, a mysterious thief who identified themselves only by the name *K* or *Kit*.

Though Kit could be a pseudonym or stand for something else, he didn't think so.

Settling back on the bed, he flipped to his notes from the Kingston situation in New York. Somewhere between the Geneva heist and the day of the curator's shooting in the museum, *The Fortunate Buddha* had made its way there. duMonde's men stalked one of the art specialists, Sophie Kingston, in a retrieval attempt.

The viscount's violence seemed to be on the rise. Despite his men's losses and the subsequent rediscovery of the item, he was in New York. *The Fortunate Buddha*, remanded to police custody, had disappeared from their evidence lockup to parts unknown.

In Sophie's file were two other notes, also secured in evidence bags. Apologies from a thief who stole her laptop, cell phone, and dissertation research—a note also signed with a *K*. So the thief remained on the trail of the Buddha and seemed the most likely candidate for removing it from police lockup. Despite the lack of video or physical evidence, Walter's gut said Kit did this.

The next file wasn't on the Buddha but the small wedding ceremony coming up in three weeks. Unlike his cousin Max's extravaganza, Pietr planned a small, informal gathering in New York with Sophie's family. Four months pregnant, they wanted to make it official before the baby came. Anya had deliberately rescheduled her own wedding to accommodate.

Anya remained one of his best assets. Despite her engagement to the son of one of IAAR's regents, she didn't turn down opportunities to reclaim stolen property and lured her fiancé along with her. The two were hopelessly besotted with each other, and he imagined it wouldn't be long before she left fieldwork behind to run assets of her own.

Regret tugged at him. A natural progression for talent, and he had done much the same thing, running assets and agents in the field rather than go after the items himself.

Until now.

Rolling his forefinger down the guest list, he paused at the one name he'd circled.

Lady Katherine Hardwicke.

The daughter of a wealthy land baron in England as well as a member of the aristocracy, she traveled in circles similar to the Sauvages. She'd also turned up in New York during the museum incident, befriended Sophie, and earned an invitation to the wedding. But these were not the facts rousing his curiosity.

No, the phone conversation he'd overheard between Sophie and the Lady Hardwicke two days prior left him intrigued.

A conversation where Sophie called Lady Katherine one name: Kit.

Beneath the invitation list lay the file he'd had pulled on Lady Katherine. Sipping his coffee, he leaned back against the pillows and read. He and Lady Katherine were about to be very well acquainted.

It was time for Jarod to get back into the game.

This one thief would not elude them again.

***

Lady Katherine Hardwicke sat at the end of a fourteen-foot-long conference table. Also present were ten of the most mind-numbingly boring bankers she'd ever met. A display on the screen scrolled through a PowerPoint presentation of the latest Hardwicke Holdings financial statements. These annual meetings killed her, but her father wanted her to know everything about the business and sent her each year to be "educated." In his opinion, the heir apparent to the Hardwicke fortune needed to be fully briefed on their holdings, their investments, when to cash out, and more. Tracing one red nail lightly against the polished mahogany, she found herself wishing for a brother.

Or four.

Her father's old-world sensibilities would have left her brothers in charge, and she could have collected her monthly stipend from the family trust. The sexist extreme didn't always carry an allure, but today it did.

The clearing of a throat dragged her attention back to the room. "Lady Hardwicke?" The elderly banker speaking was Fitzhugh. Miles Fitzhugh had been one of her father's personal financial advisors for over a quarter of a century. He looked down his nose at her, probably still seeing her in polka-dotted dresses and pigtails from childhood.

"Yes, Mr. Fitzhugh?" She fought to wipe the glazed expression from her eyes and focused on the man at the head of the table.

"I wanted to make sure you were paying attention." If any other man at the table spoke to her in that manner, she might have bristled. But Miles couldn't see her as an adult, so she often granted him the tolerance due an elder.

Often, but not always. "The third quarter decline has been offset by our fourth quarter earnings. Overall, the annual financial loss statement is significantly improved over the last fiscal year, but if we rearrange our investments, withdraw from energy, and reinvest in local economies—particularly the booming green movements and organic foods sections in the Midwest—we could see a long-term gain within five years."

Several of the bankers went from smirking to studying the portfolios in front of them. Two coughed, and a third turned away to sneeze, while one of the younger, more unfamiliar bankers sitting near the center of the table watched her. She could almost smell the curiosity in his expression.

"Of course, if we remove our investments from energy, we lose the potential gain in the new hybridization movements developing in Japan and Germany. Our Italian investment, for example, has completed a prototype for a solar-powered electric vehicle. Our partner in Norway is working on a refined version of an electric car battery which will not need to be replaced annually but may last for up to five years. Instead of pulling money from any of these projects, we would see a greater return in facilitating introductions, supporting future development, and reaping the rewards of fiscally sound electric vehicles."

Miles' wrinkled face bloomed into a grin. "We could, Lady Hardwicke. But it's a gamble."

"True. So let's take it a step further. Two presentations ago, you mentioned the application of wind farm technology to greenhouse organics in New Mexico. Why not increase our investment, take the gains we've made up in the last quarter toward funding not only these energy and transportation projects, but also the organic food movement? By diversifying, we can offset losses in one area with gains in another and continue to promote cleaner, more efficient vehicles and healthier food sources."

Ambrose Bingham rapped his knuckles against the table. He and Miles were her father's favorite advisors. But, if Miles said blue sky, Ambrose would argue it was red. They were diametrically opposed across the board. "Lady Hardwicke," he began, his voice filled with patient disdain. "You may think throwing good money after bad in an industry which continues to report losses twenty years after developing on the fringe is a 'gamble,' but it's a fool's bet.

You will lose money in all three areas you've mentioned."

"Huge gobs?" She lifted her brows and leaned back in the chair. Crossing one leg over the other, she pasted on a patient expression. "Armored car loads of cash? Or pennies on a spreadsheet accumulating into a respectable tax write-off at the end of the quarter?"

The Hardwicke family fortune amounted to billions, not millions. Small, medium, and large investments in multiple industries, charities, and private start-ups diversified their interests. They maintained healthy sums in every country where they did business and worked diligently to stay within regulation. But, at the end of the day, the final decisions always rested with her father—or, in cases like this, when he appointed her his representative—her.

"Well, it might take some research...." Ambrose hedged.

"No, it doesn't." Miles scented the blood in the water and leaned in for the kill. "We've already shown a 3 percent gain overall each quarter we diversified, offsetting any loss—"

"But if we removed the losing investments, those proving capital losses in the last four consecutive quarters...." Ambrose fired back, and, within a minute, the two men began flinging figures at each other as though old-world duelists, trying to cut each other down with the facts. It didn't take long for the rest of the bankers to jump in, throwing their support to one side or the other.

Kit rubbed the side of her nose and tried to swallow the satisfaction. When they yelled at each other, they ignored her. Oddly, though, one man at the table seemed less interested in the debate than in staring at her.

The new banker.

Paulson?

Perkins?

Parker.

His last name was Parker. She didn't recall if Miles used a first name when he'd gone around the table. Mid-thirties, dark, close-cropped hair, a strong chin, and very firm lips quirked with amusement. He noticed her attention and flicked a look at the chaos around the table before tipping his head.

She considered accepting the accolade but merely widened her eyes in mock innocence. His grin edged the corners of his mouth wider and turned him from moderately attractive to truly handsome. Awareness shivered over her skin, and she forced herself to look away.

Miles rapped the table. The chatter muted immediately. He rose and planted both hands on the table. "This is a pointless debate. Our task is to apprise Lady Hardwicke of the facts, present prospectus reports, and offer our suggestions. Everything else is moot."

Grumbling met his statement, but the bankers leaned back in their chairs as though attempting to soothe their own ruffled feathers. Miles stared at her down the length of the table.

"Lady Hardwicke, do you feel you have been briefed fully?"

"To a point." She gave her father's old friend a lazy nod. "But I would like full financial statements for the Italian and Norwegian investments as well as the proposed property development in Dubai." The man to her immediate right jerked at the last. She could almost smell his surprise and delight at the request. He'd brought up the construction deals in Dubai at the beginning of the meeting—nearly four hours before—and been drowned out almost unanimously by the others.

Miles frowned. "Very well. We'll have the full reports compiled and sent to your hotel."

"Fantastic." She rose from the chair, flipped her digital tablet off, and slid it into her oversized bag. Every man at the table rose, but it was Parker's regard she caught herself watching. Speculation joined amusement in his expression. "Thank you, gentlemen. As always, it's been a pleasure. I will see you all again next year."

She slid a card out of her wallet and handed it to the man on her right—Kevin Donner. "Mr. Donner." She pulled his attention as the others gathered their things together, shut down laptops, and repacked their briefcases. "Please send all of your information to me directly."

He took the card with a quick thanks and a flash of relief. Miles hated his plan. She adored the old man, but he would take his time to review, tweak, change, and force Donner to backtrack on his suggestions, and it would be months before she received anything.

"Yes, ma'am. Thank you, ma'am."

"You're welcome." Slipping the strap of her purse over her shoulder, she made the rounds of the table, deliberately choosing the side opposite Parker. Glad-handing was part of the job. She spared a comment for each man, asking about a wife, a child, or a hobby. She always made sure to brush up on the little tidbits before every meeting. She knew how to leave a good impression, reminding even the most staid banker she cared. Her father believed in earning respect and courting affection, traits she'd practiced from an early age.

Miles took her arm as she reached him, leaving his things for his assistant to gather. Cane in hand, he led her from the room. A flash of frustration shone in his eyes and his mouth tightened, the expression, so fleeting, she might have imagined it.

"So, Katherine. How is your father these days?" Miles tucked her hand into the crook of his arm. She slowed her pace to match his uneven gait.

"Retired and enjoying it—mostly."

"I still can't believe he's stepping down."

Don't believe or don't like it? "Monica encourages him to take it easy, but don't think he's completely out. He reviews every file, every report, and if he wants changes, he asks for them."

"Oh. Good. Good." Miles patted her hand. At the elevator, she reached out, pressed the button, and dropped a kiss on his withered cheek.

"Don't worry, Miles. I won't run Hardwicke into the ground. Daddy wouldn't let me." Her tone was light, placating, and teasing, but the spike of guilt shining in Miles' eyes told her she'd read his concern correctly. He didn't want Daddy's little girl destroying all of Daddy's hard work.

"Now, Katherine…you know I trust your instincts and your education." The elevator dinged open, and they stepped inside. Whether out of respect for Miles or a desire to not be dragged into the further conversation, the others left them to the privacy of the elevator.

Too bad. She'd hoped Parker would at least follow.

The doors closed, and Miles shed the grandfather attitude. "But you lead with your heart, and emotional decisions are bad for business, dear."

She preferred the blunt honesty. "And, yet, we're still showing a profit. Your retirement and fortunes are guaranteed, Miles. Times are changing. Hardwicke needs to change with them and stay in front of the cutting edge or risk being sliced in half when it progresses without us."

"Young lady…." His cheeks popped with the force of his breath, and his face flushed. "My point, exactly. You want to gamble on every new idea out there, and some are downright foolish. What

Donner wants to do is mire us in the Middle East. Never a good plan for success."

"Ten years ago? Probably not. But Dubai is a capitalist boomtown with multiple opportunities for legacy and investment." She bit down on the next words. Old-fashioned and mired in the past as he may be, she did genuinely like the old man. "Look, I asked to see his plans. I want to get a good feel for what he is seeing. Maybe he's got ideas and connections we don't. I didn't agree to anything."

"Hmmph." Miles folded both hands on top of the cane and leaned on it. "Don't try to placate me. You're going to listen to everything I say, nod respectfully, and go do whatever the hell it is you want."

Laughter rippled through her, and she was still chuckling when the express elevator dinged open on the ground floor. Despite his infirmities, she led the way out because Miles wouldn't have it any other way. Pressing another kiss to his cheek, she winked. "How about I promise to discuss it with you before I do what I want to do?"

"It's better than nothing." He returned the buss to her cheek and patted her arm. "Give my regards to your father and remind him he owes me for our last poker game."

"Yes, sir." Another wink and she pivoted on her heel to head across the lobby. Midtown Manhattan hummed with foot traffic, cars, and tourists. Her limo waited out front. If she hurried, she could be at LaGuardia in a couple of hours and, after weeks of delay, finally be on her way to Los Angeles.

A very masculine hand caught the door to the vestibule and pulled it open. Startled, she glanced to find Parker smiling at her. His easy expression didn't quite reach his eyes. "Mr. Parker...."

"Lady Hardwicke." His voice lacked any discernible accent but possessed a distinctly masculine quality, low and direct. He motioned her through the door and followed her. He caught the second door to the street, opening it as well.

Traffic noise spilled over them as they stepped out onto the sidewalk. "You handled those men very, very well up there."

She appreciated the compliment. "Thank you. You didn't seem to have much to add to the conversation."

"It wasn't a conversation." The right corner of his mouth curved with a hint of wryness. "Or, at least, that wasn't their plan. They wanted to brief you, have you sign off, and move on."

She nodded, bemused he'd noticed. She walked over to the limo and handed her purse to the driver who opened the back door and stowed it inside. "It's what they usually expect, although I've never done what's usually expected of me."

"I liked it. You handled all of it gracefully. But why Dubai?" He canted his head, curiosity in his tone, not criticism.

She wore four-inch heels and still had to look up at him. Crossing her arms, she considered ignoring his question and asking him to join her for the ride to the airport and drinks along the way. But she never mixed business and pleasure.

Well, almost never....

He wore no ring on his left hand and no tan line betrayed the recent presence of one. But it wouldn't be the first time a married man decided to forgo the wedding band.

"Why not Dubai?" She turned the question back on him. "It's a wealthy region, plenty of opportunities, multiple construction projects, and booming Western interests."

"Because it's a glut, too. You're not looking at creating anything new or cutting edge as you explained to Miles. So is Dubai a distraction to focus them elsewhere and rile them up at the same time?"

Intrigued, she arched both brows and closed the gap between them to less than a foot. "Why would I want to distract them?"

"So you can close the deal you really want and then make a peace offering by conceding to their wishes."

Her belly fluttered. *Oh, hello, Mr. Intelligent and Sexy. The combination should be illegal.* "Interesting supposition. What deal do you think I'm really after?" If only she planned to stay in the city for another few nights, she might be able to explore the depths of this man—or at least find out if he was married.

"You didn't comment on the Costa Rica proposal at all. In fact, you distracted them with a colorful golf joke and derailed the entire conversation for an hour."

A warning tingle raced up her spine. "Clever deduction, but maybe I like golf."

Parker laughed, a hard, delicious sound which caressed her. Excitement curled in her chest. "Must explain why you stared off into space when they debated the last Master's."

Did he watch me through the whole meeting? She rifled her

memory for what areas of their organization he represented but couldn't place him. "I learned a long time ago, it's good business to not disagree with the men you're talking to, particularly about their favorite sports." She made a show of glancing at her watch, even though she knew the exact time. "I have a flight in a couple of hours. Would you like to join me for drinks on the way to the airport? My driver can take you wherever you need to be after."

"I would enjoy the time." He motioned to the car.

Ronald, her driver, gave her a mildly amused look as she slid past him and into the car. She scooted over the seat and moved her purse before Parker joined her.

Leaning back, she crossed her legs, very well aware the skirt rode up and with no table between them now. "So, tell me about Costa Rica, Mr. Parker, and why you think it's the deal I should be interested in?"

Amusement creased his face. "Jarod."

"I'm sorry?" She played dumb easily enough—paint on a pretty smile, lift her brows, and blink. Most men bought it.

"Jarod Parker." He held out his hand, and she grasped it. "But please, call me Jarod."

Electricity skated over her palm at the warm contact. His fingers closed on her hand, and she realized how large a man he was. *Appearances really can be so deceiving....* "All right, Jarod. Call me Katherine."

He matched her smile and raised the ante, holding her hand hostage. "Would you mind Kat?"

"Actually, I prefer Kit."

"Kit." He rolled the name around on his tongue. Her gaze went unerringly to his mouth. What else could he do with his tongue? "Kit Kat—I like it."

Her face warmed. Dear God, was she blushing? Clearing her throat, she extracted her hand. "I prefer Kit, but I reserve it only for my friends. So you may call me Katherine." Time to get some distance and perspective.

"Whatever you say, Kit Kat." He settled back against the seat, and the tingles radiating out from her middle increased.

Oh. My.

Chapter Two

L ady Hardwicke wasn't what he'd expected when he leveraged an invitation to the meeting with her financial advisors. Miles Fitzhugh dabbled in the traffic of stolen artwork—enough to have had his hands slapped by the IAAR more than once. His latest fiasco included a Raphael—valuable enough, they could have sent him to a plush prison cell for the rest of his life. The IAAR gave Fitzhugh a choice, return the Raphael and cooperate with a future "favor" or face criminal charges.

The wealthy banker blustered and argued, but, like all the powerful men before him, caved at the idea of facing a real consequence to his actions. Using his Walter Curry identity, Jarod sent an email briefly introducing Jarod Parker to him and the orders to allow him to attend the meetings. When he arrived earlier in the day, Fitzhugh had barely said a word to him—simply vouched him through the door and all but ran in the other direction.

Jarod didn't mind the lack of support. In fact, he preferred it. The lengthy meeting detailing every financial dollar of Hardwicke's extensive investments provided him with the perfect opportunity to observe Katherine—Kit.

"Drink?"

"Water." No point in alcohol. He wanted all his wits about him...and her if he were to be honest.

"Mr. Parker?" She held out a bottle of water to him. If his request for water surprised her, she didn't show it. She, too, chose one of the small bottles. The limo glided through New York traffic, muffling the noise beyond and leaving them cocooned in privacy.

"Jarod," he reminded her, brushing her hand with his as he

took the bottle. Her skin felt like satin, and he wondered if it was as silky everywhere. "We covered this already."

"We did, but before I knew you wanted something from me." She twisted off the bottle cap and tipped it up for a long drink. He stared a moment too long at the way her lips pressed against the opening and longer still at her throat when she swallowed.

Business first. He opened his own bottle. "And you are presuming I want something from you."

"Yes, I am." She leaned back against the plush seat, uncrossing and re-crossing her legs. She screwed the cap back on slowly. "But, then, you sought me out."

Amusement curled through him. "You're basing the assumption on what?"

"I rode the executive express elevator down to the lobby. You were still in the room when Miles and I left. So you had to have taken the second express elevator to the third floor and jogged down the stairs." She waved lightly with one manicured hand. "Not that I'm not flattered, but you also didn't have any business proposals or finances for me to approve or review during the meeting. So what is it you want from me, *Mr. Parker*?"

Desire flooded through humor, but he refrained from uttering the first provocative words springing to mind. *Business always.* Too long a player in this game, one elegant lady with her sweet curves and seductive power would not distract him from his goal.

"Maybe I wanted to spend time with a beautiful, intelligent woman." He took a drink of the water as though still mulling the possibilities. "Maybe I wanted a chance to ask you what you wanted so I could dazzle you at the next investors meeting."

"Or maybe you wanted to find out if I am as loose as the gossip columnists like to report...." She shifted, leaning forward. The white jacket she wore over the deeper green silk shirt parted, giving him a lovely view of creamy white breasts pushing up against the plunging neckline of her blouse. "After all, you're exactly my type. Dark. Handsome. Brooding. Maybe a touch of mystery."

The words stroked his cock, and he forced himself to stay relaxed against the seat. She sat an arm's length away, and her calf-length skirt possessed the most wicked of slits all the way up to her thigh. It wouldn't take much to push it up and....

He choked the thought off. Maybe he had been out of the game too long. "Do you want to have sex with me?" Not the question

Jarod intended to ask, but the surprise and delight flaring beneath the suspicion in her gaze rewarded the impulse.

"Are you married?" The counter question surprised him. He didn't wear a ring, didn't even have a tan line.

"No." He shook his head once.

"Ever been married?"

His mouth curved with unexpected enjoyment, humor tying with desire on the mad dash through his system. "No."

"Excellent."

She set her water bottle down and leaned back against the seat. He regretted the lack of visible cleavage, but not even its lack could quiet the almost inaudible hunger rousing inside. *Pay attention.* He needed his wits active, not his libido.

"You didn't answer my question." He should probably let it go, move them on to more relevant topics—like where she planned to fly today and whether she'd stolen the Buddha.

"Hmm." She reached into her purse and pulled out a small compact. "Apparently not."

He enjoyed the front row seat to her next performance. And it *was* a performance, he had no doubt. She flipped open a compact, checked her makeup, and applied a sheer gloss to her already red lips. Her tongue even came out to swipe at her lower lip, the barest hint of a caress. His cock swelled uncomfortably at the gesture. She snapped the compact closed and took her time before looking at him again.

"Are you playing with me?" he asked before she could say anything.

Her mouth curved, and her chin lifted. "Maybe."

"Care to share the rules, or do you prefer I guess?"

She stroked a finger against the seat next to her. A single gesture, her nail gliding over the soft fabric, and the need in him turned up another notch. Despite the comfort of the suit he wore, heat burned him up from the inside. If her plan involved driving him wild, she succeeded.

Lady Katherine Hardwicke was a far more dangerous opponent than he'd anticipated.

Her white teeth threatened to graze the fresh gloss on her lips, and he couldn't tear his gaze away. "Rules are for children."

"And fair play," he countered. "If you break a rule, you serve a penalty. If you break a rule, you deserve the consequences."

"How can there be consequences if there are no rules?" Her nails clicked together as she rubbed her thumb against her fore and middle fingers. "Money buys a lot of latitude, but even the wealthy have to follow certain rules—protocols if you will."

"So this is about privilege?" He couldn't pinpoint where she headed with this discourse, but tension corded his body. He wanted to know.

He really wanted to know.

"Why does it have to be about anything, Mr. Parker?"

He could learn to loathe the way his name sounded on her lips—too formal, too stilted, too at a distance.

"Because, Kit Kat, it's absolutely about something. You think I want something. You in turn have something to conceal...or maybe you want something, too. You ask me if I want to have sex with you—" He broke off, and Kit threw her head back and laughed.

God what a gorgeous laugh: rich, throaty, and filled to the brim with utter delight. It captivated him more swiftly than her decadent curves or provocative actions. Her green eyes sparkled in the light filtering through the tinted windows. Her wonderful lips spread into a true smile—not the pasted on polite facsimile she affected during the meeting, but an honest, cheek-cramping grin.

Holy shit, I do want to have sex with her. He wanted it, and it distracted him. He'd asked her, not the other way around. Her unfiltered joy at his discomfiture and mistake made it hard to regret, though.

"Point to you." He inclined his head.

"Only one point?" She folded her arms beneath her breasts. "So, the answer to your question, Mr. Parker, will have to wait until you earn the right to ask it again."

Again.

He could work with the promise of further opportunities.

"And when would that be, Kit Kat?" He didn't miss the faintest twitch at the corner of her mouth each time he called her by the new nickname. Her mouth may have declared she didn't like it, but her actions said otherwise.

"That would be telling, wouldn't it?'

And so, they played this game on multiple levels. He glanced out the window. They were in Queens, on the road toward La Guardia.

"You're flying somewhere."

"Yes. Too easy, Jarod. I already told you I had a flight...." Her turn to trail off.

He shrugged. "Point to me."

"So it would seem."

Her accent embraced his name, rolling it around her tongue to make it sound almost exotic. Intoxication—Lady Katherine Hardwicke—pure intoxication, and the intoxicated made foolish mistakes. He would do well to remember the dangers and forgo imbibing.

But damn, he couldn't imagine anything smoother or sweeter than the woman sitting across from him.

"Well, at least I'm still in the game." He sat forward, elbows braced lightly on his knees.

"Did you have some doubts you could keep up?"

"With you, Kit Kat?" His turn to be pleased. "None whatsoever."

Traffic thinned as they rolled into the airport. He glanced out the window, considering.

"Are you a determined man, Jarod?" She exhaled the question.

"Very."

"Good."

They weren't talking about sex anymore.

"Good?" He watched her from the corner of his eye, keeping his head turned toward the window.

The warmth in her smile dimmed, and sadness flickered through her expression. "Yes. Determined men don't give up. They fight for what they want. They challenge those around them to be better, go farther."

Really? "Do you need to be challenged, Kit Kat?"

The limo rolled to a stop, and she set her water bottle down. The driver opened the door and let the noise of arriving and departing planes into the cool, dark interior.

"Yes, Jarod." She brushed her hand against his leg as she scooted to the door and stepped out, purse around her arm. The driver reached in and claimed her other bag. For the barest of moments, the mask slipped and a vulnerable woman gazed down at him. "I very much need a challenge."

As quickly as the glimpse appeared, it vanished, and she covered her gorgeous eyes with a pair of sunglasses. "Until next time. My driver will take you wherever you need to go." She pivoted and walked away, her expensive heels clicking against the concrete.

The driver glanced down at him.

"Give me a minute," he told the man.

The driver nodded and closed the door. Jarod thumbed on his phone and checked the report.

He'd cloned her phone while they rode. He chose calendar and looked at her flight plans. Shutting the phone off, he tapped the window. The door opened.

"Destination, sir?"

Jarod climbed out, his bottle of water still in hand. No sense in leaving it behind for fingerprints. He didn't expect she'd run him, but his training didn't allow for anything less. "I'm here. Turns out I need to fly to Los Angeles."

The driver's flashfire amusement told him he got it right. Los Angeles was exactly where Lady Hardwicke headed.

"Good luck, sir. You're going to need it."

He waved to the man and strode inside.

Credentials and a private plane waiting sped Kit through security. Her bag included a laptop, a digital tablet, and her current book. Everything she needed was either on the plane or at her hotel in Los Angeles. She'd sent her luggage ahead earlier in the morning before leaving for her meeting. She met her pilot and co-pilot at the gangway to her jet. They would file their flight plan and request a departure time. Stripping off her jacket, she walked on board the flying fortress her father had invested fifteen million to re-outfit as a luxury apartment for the skies. Dismissing her crew to their workstations, she closed the door between the working cabin and the bedroom.

In the bedroom, she hung her jacket in the closet with the collection of outfits ranging from the used and needs-to-go and the freshly returned and still in its plastic from the cleaners. Unbuttoning her blouse, she strolled into the bathroom and started the shower. Fifteen minutes later, she stood under the warm spray, rinsing off the day of meetings, and the growing restlessness. Finally, she could leave New York and finish the job that had taken her nearly two years to complete.

If she could have managed it, she would have bolted from New York months ago, but her father's business commitments tied her to the city. The nervous knots in her stomach twisted tighter. She'd been running down the clock for months. What began as a simple effort to fulfill a dying wish had turned into an obsession—and clusterfuck—of epic proportions.

Anger rasped over her nerves, and she clenched her fists. The violent urge to pound them on the wall took time to drain away. Tears soaked her cheeks, but she turned her face into the spray and washed them off even as they fell. Tears of frustration. Tears of anger.

Tears of grief.

It didn't matter. Lady Katherine Hardwicke didn't cry—at least not in public—and she certainly didn't bang her fists against the wall or rail against God. She'd chosen this path, and if she were at all honest with herself, even knowing where it would take her, she wouldn't have chosen differently.

"Please hang on until I get there," she whispered, half in prayer and half in plea. It was too late to shake off the melancholy, so she settled for scrubbing her face until her skin felt raw and her hair until it squeaked.

She let the excess of emotion sluice away with the soap and stood under the spray until the gentle chime of the captain ringing through to the apartment sounded. Shaking herself out of the reverie, she twisted the water off and slid the tiny door open. Towel wrapped around her, she flipped the intercom button.

"Yes, Captain?"

"We have clearance to depart in ten minutes. Are you ready for us to pull away from the gate?"

"Yes, thank you, Captain. I'll be in my seat directly."

"Yes, ma'am. We're set to arrive in Los Angeles at 10:00 p.m. local time. Would you like to stay on the plane until morning?"

"We'll see." It depended on whether she could sleep. She would prefer deplaning immediately, picking up her car, and driving north. But it was better to make her decisions on the fly for the time being.

The pilot murmured an acknowledgement, and the intercom went silent. She toweled off and changed into a pair of plaid cotton pajama bottoms and a dark-green tank top. Carrying the brush with her, she chose a chair in the bedroom and strapped on her seat belt. When the pilot announced they would be taking off, she leaned back and brushed her damp hair.

Fifteen minutes later, they reached their cruising altitude and the seat belt sign blinked off. It was after eight o'clock local time, and hunger assaulted her. Her red curls were still damp, but she pulled them back into a ponytail. She would have to style her hair in the morning, but she didn't need to bother on a flight where both attendants had known her since she was a pimply faced teenager flying back and forth to boarding school.

The scent of salmon and fresh coffee greeted her when she opened the door.

The man sitting at the table—set for two, coincidentally enough—sent her pulse rabbiting.

"Mr. Parker." *What the hell is he doing here?* Little startled her and even less surprised her. Jarod Parker did both.

Twice in the same day.

First, when he flirted with her in the limo and she found it so difficult to maintain her distance and now here, on her plane—at altitude.

"Good evening, Kit Kat. Enjoy your shower?" He rose and circled the table to turn out the chair he obviously meant for her to sit in. He'd abandoned his jacket and the tie. The deep-amber of his dress shirt matched his warm-brown eyes to perfection. The shirt opened three buttons at the collar and revealed a hint of the chest beneath.

"Why are you on my plane?" She didn't bother trying to retrieve the game right now. He had her at a complete disadvantage. She stood there without cosmetics, suit, or hairstyle. Her pajamas felt almost too sheer under the heat of his gaze. She suspected the shrewdness she'd glimpsed in him earlier was but the tip of a very deep iceberg.

"Well, I'm about to have dinner with a very lovely lady. Or, at least, I hope I am." The corner of his far-too-kissable mouth turned up in a hint of play. "Of course, you probably mean why am I on board to begin with?"

She folded her arms and waited. Her insides jittered like a roadrunner on a caffeine buzz, but she kept her outward calm and focused. It didn't matter about standing there barefoot in a tank top that didn't disguise her nipples' tingling reaction to his presence. It sure as hell didn't matter if the first thought she had on seeing him was what he would look like without the shirt.

Warning bells clanged in her head. Their first encounter on the curb, no matter how he tried to play it, smelled of contrivance.

His presence on her plane—conspiracy theories bloomed from fewer facts.

Jarod held up both hands, palms outward, and circled around the dining table to the forward-facing chairs. He retrieved his briefcase from beneath the seats and clicked it open. He glanced at her twice, making sure she could see his hands at all times, and pulled out a folder.

The standard manila folder, with no names or labels to distinguish it from any other, was thick—nearly an inch thick.

"You left the Costa Rica project notes in your limo. I tried to catch up with you, but you were already aboard. I explained to the captain and showed him my credentials. He called Fitzhugh, who vouched for me. Since I also have business in Los Angeles, I didn't think you'd mind the company...or the additional challenge."

The plausible explanation threatened to take the wind out of her outrage, but it didn't budge her suspicions or silence the clang of alarm in her mind. She didn't like too many coincidences.

She held out her hand and said nothing. He offered her another smile, but not as easily nor with as much humor. He looked worried.

Good.

She carried the folder and retreated to the side to pick up a phone. "Captain, please ring me through to Miles Fitzhugh."

The captain completed the call while she kept her gaze on Jarod. The folder contained exactly what he said it did. The facts and figures of the Costa Rican deal—a folder she had put into her bag in the conference room. She didn't make mistakes in business, and she hadn't opened her things during the limo ride.

He would have to be pretty slick to have filched it right under her nose.

Miles answered the phone on the third ring. "Fitzhugh."

"Miles, it's Katherine." She assumed the smooth, mildly flirtatious tone she often used with her father's older business executives—it placated and tempted at the same time.

"Good evening." He sounded worried.

He should be.

"Yes, could you please explain to me why Jarod Parker is aboard my plane?"

The awkward silence followed by Miles' pained cough told her he hadn't wanted to agree to this, or was, at the very least, mildly embarrassed. She waited, allowing him a moment to gather his composure. Jarod leaned against the table, hands resting against it in relaxed fashion. But, despite his posture, his eyes narrowed and the corners of his mouth tightened.

"I'm sorry, Katherine. I should have warned you. Your father...." He hesitated.

Her father.

Dammit!

"I see. He put you up to this?"

Miles went silent, probably out of a thirty-year relationship personally and professionally with Lord Hardwicke. "In a manner of speaking."

"It's all right, Miles," she soothed, repeating his name. It had always seemed to do the trick in the past, and this was no exception. "I'm sure Mr. Parker will be perfectly respectable company for the flight, and I appreciate your honesty."

At the next stretch of silence, she let the old man off the hook. Her father's interest in her marriage prospects had taken a deplorable rise over the last year. He'd teased her with a dozen potential matches at various parties across Europe. When she started avoiding him at parties, he'd thrown two at her via professional engagements.

She stared across the cabin at sexy candidate number three.

At least her father's taste seemed to be improving.

"Have a good evening, Miles."

"Absolutely." Relief swamped the man's voice. "You as well, Katherine. Until next time."

They rang off, and she carried the folder to the table. Jarod straightened and held her chair out for her again. She gave him a long, studying look.

Setting the file down, she leaned back in the chair. The flight attendants joined them, opening the serving seals and pouring the wine. They were efficient and quiet, although Cindy, the older of the two women, gave her a wink and a thumbs-up behind Jarod's back. The staff approved of her father's efforts.

Too bad she couldn't really enjoy them at the moment.

When they were alone, she picked up her wine. "You should understand, Mr. Parker, this isn't going to end well for you."

"Oh?" He lifted his brows.

"Absolutely not." She sipped the wine. It didn't matter he was sexy as hell. If her father thought sending every potentially advantageous businessman in her direction a good idea, then it would be better not to get his hopes up.

Or hers.

He ignored his wine glass and prodded the salmon with his fork. It flaked perfectly. But, then, it would. The staff didn't know how to serve an ill-cooked meal. "I'm going to suppose it is another facet of our game." He lifted the forkful to his mouth and nodded slightly as he tasted it.

"You may suppose whatever you like. I am not in the habit of letting others choose who shares my bed." She swirled the wine in her glass. She hadn't eaten since the boxed lunches during the meeting, and even then she'd only picked at her food.

He choked and coughed, reaching for the wine to wash down the bite. "I beg your pardon?"

"Mr. Parker, in all games, there is a time to drop the charade. Miles ratted you out." She took a second, longer swallow of the wine and put it aside. The warmth spreading through her belly had less to do with the alcohol than her company, but she had better eat if she wanted to drink any more.

"And exactly what did he say?" The caution in Jarod's voice brought her head up, and she stared at him.

The tension in his face returned. A muscle ticked in his jaw. The better tell was his hands, though. They went completely still, even as the knuckles whitened where he gripped the silverware. *I wonder what debt or favor Daddy is holding over his head. I'll have to find out. Or, if he proves a nuisance, maybe I'll let Daddy hang him out to dry with it.*

"He told me why he gave you the authorization to be on the plane." She cut into her own fish. "So enough with the games. It's a long flight. You can take the sofa over there, and, when we land at LAX, you can be on your way."

He sat silently. She forced herself to eat three bites of the salmon in quick succession, followed by a forkful of the steamed spinach and grilled zucchini. Her lack of appetite did not do the meal justice, but her audience forced her to play the part. Their air of civility wore on her. She'd rather be curled up, snacking on her dinner in bed and watching the latest movies she'd missed thanks to the whirlwind schedule she'd been maintaining.

But, no. She sat at a table with a perfectly respectable, smoking-hot-should-be-licked-often stranger. Damn her father.

Hell, if her father hadn't sent him, she could have indulged in one of those carnal impulses which used to land her in the scandal rags during her university years. When the heat in her body continued to spread, warming her cheeks and breasts, she reached for the wine again. Maybe a glass or three would knock the temperature off her libido.

"You seem very relaxed, considering our present circumstances." He sounded almost curious.

"I'm used to it." She sighed and ran her tongue along her teeth, hoping no bits of veggie were embarrassing her. "Unfortunately."

"Well, if you're used to it, maybe you should consider a change in careers." The odd comment, coupled with his pursed lips, dragged her attention away from her raging hormones to stare at him again. He watched her with no attempt to disguise the shrewd predator in his eyes. A fresh wave of awareness rolled over her.

He wasn't any ordinary businessman, and his attempts at vanilla engagement, from his relaxed dress to his mannerisms, couldn't disguise the difference anymore. Something far more dangerous than an unwanted matchmaking attempt lurked in his gaze.

Intrigue and wariness clashed inside.

"Why would I change careers? I'm destined to inherit the entire organization. I have to know how it works from top to bottom. Or are you one of those men who thinks marrying me will be your key to the executive office, and I'll be at home hosting tea while popping out the requisite heirs?"

Jarod tugged his ear then set his utensils down. "Kit Kat, what the hell are you talking about?"

"My father, *Mr. Parker*. And stop calling me by that horrid nickname." Irritation rose to the top of her desire and flamed. "I asked you to call me Katherine."

"No. You told me to. I prefer Kit Kat. It suits your mercurial moods. What does your father have to do with my being on this plane?"

"Everything." She leaned forward. "Miles told me Daddy sent you to the meeting and here. I am used to my father's matchmaking—although he's generally a great deal subtler than this. I suppose my birthday last month and the engagements of several of his associates' children has him thinking."

"Miles told you I'm here as a—"

"Seriously, Mr. Parker? A stud service. Yes, my father sent you to stand stud for his recalcitrant princess who will not settle down.

Granted, you're an exceptionally fine specimen, but I have no desire to wear the reins which undoubtedly go with your promising physique."

Jarod's mouth opened briefly then snapped shut. To her amazement—and ire—he started to laugh.

"What's so funny?"

"You're not mad your father might have sent me, Kit Kat. You're mad you wanted me, and now you think you can't have me."

She sat up straighter in the chair, aggravation dragging its nails across the chalkboard of her spine. "I am glad I amuse you." She tossed her napkin onto the plate, all pretense of appetite gone. Standing, she gave him a practiced look of dismissal. "Good evening, Mr. Parker. I expect you off my plane as soon as we land in Los Angeles."

She didn't make it two steps away from the table before he caught her arm and spun her back. She impacted against his chest, and her hands flattened against a very hard, very well-developed set of pectoral muscles, his mouth an inch from her own. "If I'm standing stud, you should at least sample the services before you dismiss them."

She wasn't sure which of them moved, but, suddenly, their mouths fused together and the heat inside of her burst into a raging forest fire. His tongue stabbed against hers, demanding and gaining access. His hand slid up to her still damp hair, and, sometime between the first caress of his tongue and the flood of want between her thighs, he released the ponytail.

The world spun, as if the private jet performed aerial acrobatics. She clung to him, fighting the waves of sensuous dizziness swarming over her and devouring every shred of common sense shrieking at her to let him go.

Who started the kiss might have been a mystery, but Jarod pulled back. He stared down at her with those deep-amber eyes. "By the way, Kit Kat…Daddy didn't send me. You sleep well tonight."

He let her go and returned to the table. He picked up his fork and knife as if nothing happened and dug into the meal. Her body sizzled, and the taste of him on her lips was far more tantalizing than the food.

Exhaling a hard breath, she turned on her heel and marched back to the door separating the bedroom from the cabin.

"Oh," his voice chased her. "I think we can call it two points for me."

Damn.

She shut the door and leaned back against it. Her pulse raced, her body trembled, and her mind quivered.

He was ahead.

Chapter Three

He finished the glass of wine and stared at the thin door standing between him and his goal. Before the flight attendants could clear the table, he wiped down the glass and the silverware. Old habits had saved his ass too many times in the past and were difficult to avoid. He accepted the offer of coffee, and the stewardesses left him with a carafe, a cup, and fresh creamer. They retreated to the front and what he imagined was their station during the flight when not needed.

An hour after their explosive kiss and her retreat to the bedroom, Jarod accepted she didn't intend to join him anytime soon. He itched to search the cabin, but it would be an exercise in futility. If she carried the Buddha personally, the priceless artifact would be in the bedroom. Retrieving his laptop, he booted up and began a casual web search of Lord Hardwicke and his impetuous daughter. He knew a great deal about Kit Kat, his thorough research uncovering several warnings from the Bridgerton Boarding Academy in Switzerland.

Katherine Hardwicke possessed a remarkable intellect. Several of her instructors commented on the difficulty of keeping the young woman engaged—and on campus. Most of the sealed records required hacking to access, but IAAR background checks remained thorough. The Hardwickes and the Sauvages shared a long acquaintance. His Kit Kat seemed linked to Pietr or Max on several occasions via newspaper speculation but—adept at reading between the lines—all Jarod found was speculation. Her romantic liaisons seemed far and few between.

At sixteen, she began appearing at her father's business

functions as his hostess. At eighteen, a noticeable three-month absence in reports of her activities intrigued him, followed by a second absence at twenty and a third one lasting nearly nine months in the year after she completed university. He would have to put a researcher on those discrepancies when they landed in Los Angeles.

At twenty-nine, she had never been engaged nor linked romantically with any one man for longer than three months. And, in spite of the rampant speculation about her affairs, no photographs or reports of in-depth emotional investment appeared, the lack of evidence more telling than all the implied assignations ascribed to the Lady Hardwicke.

Pouring another cup of coffee, he studied the closed door as though it might reveal prize clues about the woman hiding behind it. Definitely hiding. He wasn't too proud to admit the electric sizzle of their kiss lingered beneath his skin, nor was he ashamed of the raw desire to push up her skimpy cotton tank top and explore the curves beneath.

His mouth quirked. He loved the pajamas. For thirty seconds, he'd seen the real Kit Kat. The freshly scrubbed, hair still damp from the shower woman with all her complicated barriers set aside when she padded barefoot out of the cabin.

Thirty seconds to appreciate the fist of need to his gut. No matter how much he told himself this was purely about business, those precious seconds gave him a glimpse of the woman beneath the polished answers and smooth handling. He saw Kit Kat.

And she was exactly who he kissed. Dragging his attention away from the door, he scrolled through the various news articles, columns, and features. He skimmed the headlines. The phone in his pocket buzzed, and he pulled it out while mulling what pieces of information were missing.

Two sentence incoming text from an asset in Geneva: *duMonde boarded a flight for the United States. Destination Los Angeles.*

He tapped out one question and hit send. *ETA?*

Swift response. *Flight scheduled to arrive at 8:00 p.m., Pacific Time.*

Dammit.

Jarod didn't believe in coincidence. duMonde was a borderline psychopath with delusions of grandeur and a definite narcissistic streak. His arrival in Los Angeles ahead of Kit disturbed him to say the least. Was she on her way to meet him?

Or had he, like Jarod, put the pieces together?

duMonde's obsession with the Buddha led to his alleged involvement in at least three deaths in New York—and the near murder of Pietr Sauvage and Jarod's most recently acquired asset to the IAAR, Sophie Kingston. Anya had a history with the French collector, one she didn't enjoy relating in her reports, but manipulating the viscount to gain access to some collections proved fruitful until his unbalanced possessive streak reared its head.

duMonde arriving LAX, 8 p.m. local time. Follow him. Fortunately, a network of worldwide assets provided him with immeasurable resources. Kit didn't need to spend any time with the French lunatic. The tough, resourceful front she exuded to the world wouldn't keep her safe.

Thumbing the phone off, he didn't examine his motivations too closely. Her complicity in the theft of *The Fortunate Buddha* did not warrant leaving her to duMonde's less than tender mercies. He'd drunk all the coffee and didn't want to ask them for more, though they were two hours from LA. The laptop screen darkened as the energy saving feature kicked in.

The Frenchman's Los Angeles trip could be completely unrelated but added a new wrinkle to the timetable. He couldn't afford to alienate Kit Kat further, not if he wanted to stay close enough to protect her. *What am I not seeing in all of this?*

A key piece of data eluded him, some fact to tie together disparate pieces of information in his possession—something that might explain Kit Kat's involvement. A woman with her level of wealth didn't dabble in stolen goods unless to purchase them. But she wasn't buying or selling the Buddha. Nothing hit IAAR's radar about an auction. Granted, the network of art fences in the world remained relatively small, but an item like the Buddha made ripples—it was how they traced them.

So what was it? What element was out of context with the rest?

Born in London, Lady Hardwicke grew up in a life of wealth and privilege. Despite modernization, British nobility still lived a step or two beyond the average British subject. They lived by a code of rules and propriety with greater allowance for flaws and eccentricities. Her private school education included four years at university studying business, management, and finance. The vanilla nature of her degree did not match the seductively provocative woman. Hardwicke Industries maintained investments in a dozen corporations worldwide. Lord Hardwicke sat on as many more boards of directors. Kit Kat assumed many of the day-to-day operational meetings in the last three years, increasing her already frequent travel schedule to a new country nearly every month.

She and her father seemed very close, but they hadn't been at the same event, or even in the same country, in months. No rumors or reports of an illness for Lord Hardwicke explained the discrepancy.

Wait a minute. He hit the spacebar on the laptop and skimmed through the headlines again. *Where the hell is her mother?*

The buzzing of the phone roused her from sleep. She blinked at the nightstand clock. It read 1:00 a.m.—had she changed it from Eastern time? Plucking the phone from the wall cradle, she tried to rub the drowsiness from her eyes. "Yes?"

"I'm sorry to wake you, Lady Hardwicke. We're about thirty minutes out and will be beginning our descent shortly. You need to move to a seat belted position." The captain's calm apology and directness pushed the fog of fatigue away.

Thirty minutes? "Did we have a delay?"

"A small one. I routed us around a storm."

"Thank you, Captain. I'll be going back to bed after we land." She hung up and dragged herself out of the tangle of sheets. The twisted bed covers spoke more to her restlessness than she imagined. Padding to the loo, the knock at the door surprised her.

Jarod.

For a few precious seconds, she'd forgotten the stowaway on board. The unpleasant jolt knocked more adrenaline into her system. She didn't open the door. "Yes?"

"The captain called back to say we'll be landing soon." Silence followed the statement and then, "I didn't want it to surprise you."

"He called me, Mr. Parker. You should pack your things and take your seat. As soon as we land and park, feel free to deplane." She yawned, and rubbed a hand against her face. "In fact, I insist."

She didn't wait for a response but walked into the loo and took care of business. Ten minutes later, she sat down on the flight chair in the room and buckled her seat belt. She could have walked out into the main cabin and dozed in one of the more comfortable seats, but this one provided more privacy.

The phone next to her buzzed. "I am buckled in, Captain," she answered in lieu of a greeting.

"Good. Plenty of room out here if you want to join me." Positively incorrigible man. Incorrigible, irritating, impertinent, and presumptuous.

So why the hell was she entertained?

"I'm perfectly comfortable where I am, Mr. Parker."

"Don't hang up." The words fell somewhere between an order and a request.

"And why shouldn't I?" Unfortunately a second yawn ruined the dare in her words.

"Because I like talking to you." The stark honesty in those six words startled and pleased her. Her lips still tingled at the memory of his kiss, and the lazy stroke of heat licking at her insides left her warm once more. Putting the event out of her mind for the second time would likely be harder than the first.

"Kit Kat?"

"I despise your use of that name." She combed her fingers through her tousled hair. He couldn't see her—her appearance didn't matter—but the effort soothed her.

"No, you don't." He laughed, the low chuckle rubbing against her senses.

"You do realize it's not polite to contradict a lady to her face." Her nose wrinkled, but her cheeks ached from grinning. Yes, her father sent him to flirt with her. Yes, he was off-limits. But, then, she'd never enjoyed being told what she could or couldn't touch. A passionate little affair might get her father off her back.

"If the lady in question wanted to join me up here, I promise not to do so to her face."

She snorted, a wholly inelegant and unladylike noise. "The lady in question is fine right where she is, and I don't believe you."

The connection ended with a click, and she barely had time to process the abrupt hang-up before a knock sounded on the door. She shook her head. Incorrigible. Pursing her lips, she was tempted to leave him waiting, but a flutter of eagerness waffled her decision in his favor.

"Come in." She hung up the phone and leaned back in her seat. She smoothed away the traces of her ridiculous smile and gathered up the mantle of composure—pajamas and rumpled bed aside. The door slid open, and he stepped inside, looking even more rakishly handsome with a faint growth of stubble and his shirtsleeves rolled up to reveal the corded muscle in his arms.

If all bankers looked like him, she would never complain about those meetings.

"I'm surprised it isn't locked." He studied her as he leaned in the doorway. The low light in the room deepened the amber appearance of his eyes.

She lifted one shoulder in a mild shrug. "I don't usually have a reason."

He glanced at the rumpled blankets then skated the same hot stare over her. Her face warmed. The impulsive need to flirt with danger left her open to reckless mistakes. One would think she had learned her lesson.

"Are you sure I can't lure you out here to join me?"

The emphasis on *lure* and *join me* teased her. She opened her mouth to tell him no but, instead, pointed to the folded-up seat across from her. "Why don't you join me?"

And there goes some of my willpower. The force of his smile devastated her need to keep him at arm's length. It should be a crime to be so damn handsome. In that moment, she hated her father—particularly because this man defied her attempts to categorize him into the look-but-don't-touch column.

"Thank you." The genuine gratitude fizzled her self-recriminations. He walked over, lowered the seat, and slid onto it. His knee brushed hers as he sat, the close confines forcing him to set one foot on either side of her legs. The warmth of him bracketed her.

"You're welcome." Her pulse took another rapid uptick.

"I'm sorry we got off to a rocky start." The apology surprised her. He leaned forward and held out a long, strong-fingered hand toward her. She considered the offer and reached over to take his hand. Screw caution. It took the fun out of living.

"I don't think our start was rocky. You boarding my plane, however...."

"Might have been pushing it. I'd plead temporary insanity, but I'd rather not discourage you any further than I have." He stroked his thumb against the back of her hand. The lightest of touches and yet it sent little sizzles of awareness up her arm with each gentle glide of his skin on hers.

"So you think you still have a chance?"

His grin appeared, and her stomach flip-flopped. "I'm almost 99 percent positive I do."

"How almost?" she asked, amused at his temerity.

"Fifty-fifty." He winked.

She laughed. "I would say you seriously rounded up, then."

"A numbers game is about perception and where you put your value."

She really should take her hand away from him, but she didn't. "So, from your perspective, your value in the positive fifty is higher than in the negative fifty?"

"No, but a snapshot isn't the full report. And I have access to the full report." The awareness zinging through her stirred up the lethargic heat from earlier. Whatever the hell else Jarod Parker might be, he was fun.

"Well, maybe I need the full report so I can make a better assessment."

"You don't read reports." He turned her hand over, continuing his sensuous little caresses against her palm. "You read people."

Surprise bit through her fascination, and she stared. An uncannily accurate observation.

Too accurate.

"I read people, too, Kit Kat. I watch those nuances of behavior, the flicker of an eyelid, the tightening of the mouth...." His voice lowered, and her pulse hammered. "The sudden intake of breath or a sharp increase in heart rate...they reveal a great deal about a person." He rubbed his thumb against her wrist. Blood pounded through her system, as if it raced down to enjoy the caress and away again.

She bit down on her lower lip and studied him. She wanted to squirm in her seat, the conflicting emotions battering her system. "And what do mine tell you?"

He leaned forward and lifted her hand to his lips. His breath whispered against her palm and sent a cascade of shivers down her spine. "You like me." Her chuckle strangled as he kissed the heel of her hand and glanced up at her, mouth poised against her flesh. "And, in case you can't tell, I like you."

The phone rang next to her, and he picked it up with his free hand and held it out to her. She accepted it, never looking away from his gaze. Her body shimmered with a fresh wave of need, desire shredding her reservations like confetti. "Yes, Captain?"

"We'll be landing in ten minutes, Lady Hardwicke."

"Thank you, Captain." She handed the phone back. He hung it

up without a word. "You said last night my father didn't send you. Truth?"

"Yes." He nodded, no prevarication, no ducking the question, no excuses. He added another kiss to her palm, and, as distractions went, it worked beautifully to scramble her thoughts.

The sensation of a controlled fall swept through her—the plane's descent. Or at least it better be. "Then, why are you on my plane, Jarod?"

His expression relaxed when she said his name, and her heart squeezed. She liked his smile.

Too much.

"I have business in Los Angeles. Important business."

"So I'm simply a means to an end?" Disappointment curdled her enjoyment.

"Yes and no."

"Wow." She blinked. "At least you're honest."

"No, not really." He rubbed her hand against his cheek. The stubble rasped her skin, but the sensation wasn't unpleasant. She should probably take issue with his casual possession, but each minute she spent with him left her curious to see where the next would take them.

She could ask him what he wasn't being honest about, but she found she would rather not know. At least not yet. "What business?"

"Arrogant French bastard." The unfiltered reply surprised her.

"I'm sorry?"

"I need to see a man about a horse. Well, in this case, a project, but he's in Los Angeles. So it's where I'm going."

"Aboard my plane."

"Yeah." He squeezed her hand as the wheels bumped against the tarmac. "Joining you was the best part. It gave me an excuse to spend more time with you."

"Uh-huh." She nibbled her lower lip. "And who is this arrogant French bastard I have to thank for your company?"

Regret seemed to shine in his eyes. So brief she might have imagined it. "Louis duMonde."

The pilot applied the brakes and the plane slowed, but her stomach continued to plummet.

Louis is in Los Angeles.... No. No. No.

She tried to control her physical reaction, but he couldn't have missed her jerk at the name or the fact she closed her eyes.

Dammit...he knows. Louis knows I have the Buddha.

"Kit Kat?" Worry coated Jarod's voice.

"Tired." She dismissed the concern before he could voice it and withdrew her hand. She missed his touch almost immediately but packed it away to be examined later. Picking up the phone, she rang the captain. "Captain, change of plans. Please have my car brought to the hanger immediately, and let's skip going to the gate."

"Yes, ma'am."

If Louis was in Los Angeles, she needed to move and move quickly. She glanced at Jarod with real regret. Cutting him off would hurt, but it would hurt a hell of a lot less than having him suffer the fate of collateral damage.

Thirty minutes later, she walked out of the airplane to find Jarod standing at the bottom of the steps, waiting for her. He gave her another one of those disarming smiles, and she shook her head. *Don't force me to be cruel.*

Headlights cut through the darkness, and she paused, one hand on the railing, to watch the vehicle pull into the hanger and park next to her car. Her heart sank.

Louis duMonde stepped out of the back of the car. In addition to Louis were his driver and a third man who remained in shadow on the passenger side of the car.

"*Bonjour, ma petite.*" Louis spread his arms wide as he strolled over to the steps.

Jarod shifted and effectively blocked Louis' access.

"Viscount. What an unexpected...." She would not say pleasure, definitely never a pleasure to see him. "Surprise."

"But shouldn't a surprise be unexpected?" Louis' gentility didn't quite touch his eyes, and the pleasant expression faltered when Jarod didn't move. "*Pardon, Monsieur. Mademoiselle* and I have much to discuss."

Her gut twisted, but Jarod didn't move. "The lady has other plans."

Louis paused, and his pleasant demeanor evaporated completely. "Oh?" His cool gaze swept up the stairs and draped her in its chill assessment. "I believe our business won't take very long, *Monsieur.* You can wait."

Unpredictable, volatile, and dangerous. Those words didn't do Louis justice. Shifting the bag against her shoulder, Kit finished her descent and slid her arm through Jarod's. If surprised by her choice, the man gave a brilliant performance because it didn't show. "Yes, Viscount duMonde, I am busy. You know better than to try and ambush me." She tsked. "And at an airport of all places. Where are your manners?"

Jarod tucked her hand into the crook of his elbow and led her toward her car, putting himself firmly between her and Louis. She appreciated the gesture, but the adrenaline flooding her system kept her wary and watchful. The two men at the car didn't move, but she could almost feel the weight of their gazes.

Louis cut around to block their path and reached out, catching her face in his cold hands, and pressed a pair of even cooler kisses to her cheeks. At her right cheek, he murmured, "Lose the boyfriend, or I'll remove him for you."

Before she could respond, Jarod hauled Louis off her and had his hand in a thumb lock. The Frenchman staggered, his face a twisted mask of pain. "Allow me to remind you, Viscount duMonde, one doesn't touch a lady unless she's invited it."

The two men at the car started in their direction.

"Jarod." Kit put a hand to his shoulder, but a glint of light bounced off metal in one of the goons' hands, and she swallowed her next words.

"You stay right there, gentlemen. I've already contacted airport security." The rasp of metal being locked and loaded echoed through the hanger accompanied the co-pilot's verbal warning. She didn't dare take her eyes off Louis' men.

Jarod glanced from the men to the co-pilot to Louis. Fury simmered in the viscount's face. "You have this?"

"Yes, sir. If you would like to go ahead and escort Lady Hardwicke, we'll take care of this," the captain answered. He'd exited on the other side of the plane and walked around her, a handgun in his hand, now trained on Louis.

"Excellent." Jarod gave Louis a little shove as he released him. The Frenchman didn't fall, but he did stumble back a few feet. He held out a hand to Kit, and she took it. Relief swamped her but didn't take the edge off her worry. "Shall we?"

"Absolutely." She found the word, surprised it didn't tremble. He led her to the car, giving the others a wide berth. So focused on them, she barely noticed when Jarod tucked her into the passenger seat, set their bags in the backseat, and circled around to slide behind the wheel. Kit never looked away from Louis.

This wasn't the first time she'd crossed him.

But the hatred on his face promised her it would be the last.

Jarod backed the car up and pulled out of the hanger ahead of the flashing security lights driving up. He reached over and put his hand on her leg. "You okay?"

She shuddered, fumbling for a way to fill the silence. "I think I messed up your meeting."

"Eh." He shrugged, and she caught a brief glimpse of his teeth flashing in the illumination from the dashboard. "I don't like to do business with assholes anyway."

She laughed.

"And now I think we're three and one, don't you?" At his smug tone, she laughed harder.

"Touché."

Chapter Four

She fell asleep, head tipped back and turned toward the window. Jarod sighed and rested his wrist against the steering wheel. They headed north and west, away from Los Angeles County. She'd said Malibu, initially, but the barest of hitch in her words after their encounter suggested to him Malibu was the first place to come to mind.

Like a cat, she didn't let little tumbles upset her. Landing on her proverbial feet, she rallied to his invasion of her plane, to the misguided belief her father sent him, and their flirtation. But duMonde?

He scared the hell out of her. Jarod wasn't sure if they were in some type of collusion when he boarded the plane to New York from London, but thirty minutes into their first meeting and he couldn't see how this self-possessed firecracker with her independent spirit and playful nature could work with a narcissistic psychopath.

Thankfully, his earlier suspicions proved wrong. But they were involved on some level...insofar as duMonde was after her. Did she steal the Buddha from him?

Thief.

The five-cent word didn't do the million-dollar woman justice. Beyond his suspicions and some circumstantial evidence, he didn't have any real proof Lady Katherine Hardwicke stole *The Fortunate Buddha.*

But she did. I know she did. duMonde suspects the same, and....
She shifted in the seat next to him, and he glanced over to see her eyes open. She covered a yawn.

"My apologies."

"No apology required." He didn't resist the urge to touch her thigh again, rubbing his knuckles against her knee lightly, soothing. "It's been a long night." Dropping the kernel of information about duMonde in her lap had allowed him to observe her reaction. Her immediate discomfort, no matter how she tried to disguise it, pleased him.

He didn't want her in business or bed with duMonde. But the lack of alliance also meant he needed to keep a warier eye out. The game over *The Fortunate Buddha* continued to escalate. The little gold statue and the promise of good luck it gave to those who rubbed its belly created so much grief in its wake.

"Jarod." She sat up, shifting her leg away. He withdrew his hand, albeit reluctantly. "I appreciate everything, but you should drive us to where you are staying and then I'll leave you to do your business in peace."

"I'd rather wait until you're safely where you need to be." Particularly since the heiress didn't travel with a bodyguard. He knew her driver in New York doubled as security, and, in Europe, she often traveled with personal guards. So why shed a layer of protection here unless she wanted to hide her activities?

"You're very sweet." The "but" hung off the end of her sentence like an accessory.

"But?" He said it for her.

"But, we just met, and, while I've thoroughly enjoyed our time together, it is time to say our good-byes." Despite the overstatement, he didn't hear a lie.

So, how do I play this? Gut reaction: find a way to stick with her. *But staying isn't about the Buddha. It's about me.* Arguably, it was also about protecting her. When duMonde put his hands on her face, all Jarod could see was how swiftly he could have snapped her neck. The French bastard was lucky Jarod hadn't broken his hand. The instinct to keep her safe ran high and contrary to his primary mission.

Thief or not, she doesn't deserve to be shot, beaten, or threatened. He flexed his fingers against the steering wheel. Letting her go to lead him to the Buddha accomplished the goal. Once he took it back, duMonde would have no reason to continue his pursuit.

As if removing the Buddha from play would stop him.

It wouldn't.

"Jarod?" Concern filtered through the question in her voice.

"I'm a little worried about the viscount's intentions." The key to a good lie rested in layering it in elements of the truth.

"Louis...." She waved a hand in the air but let go of whatever thread of story she was about to share. "You don't have to worry about him. Now I'm aware he's in the area, I can avoid him."

"He had two armed men with him, Kit Kat. I don't think he wants to be avoided." He controlled his inflections, too pushy and she'd resist. Too blasé and she might not take the threat seriously. If she hadn't left for Los Angeles immediately following the meeting, he would be more embedded with her.

"The viscount likes to throw his weight around, but he's nothing for you to worry about. I won't be in the area long. In fact, I planned to drive north after we landed, hence the car."

"How far north?"

"We have a house in Malibu."

Lips quirking at how she clung to her earlier diversion, he swallowed a chuckle. Malibu wasn't an answer or her destination, but she did speak the truth. "Okay, how about a compromise?"

"I'm listening." Amusement softened the hint of warning in her tone.

"I'll take you to the house in Malibu. Make sure you're behind locked gates, as it were, and then I'll head out." He held up a finger when she opened her mouth as if to agree. Glancing at her, he grinned. "If...you agree to have dinner with me when you're back in Los Angeles."

"I didn't say anything about coming back to Los Angeles." She avoided the question. "And you live in New York."

"Fine, agree to have dinner with me in L.A., New York, London—wherever." He gritted his teeth at the slip but forced his hands to stay relaxed. The darkness offered him a cloak of sorts from her all-too-observant eyes, but passing cars illuminated the interior regularly.

"You are a determined man, Jarod." She leaned her head back against the seat.

"Not a no." He followed the highway curve to head toward Malibu.

"True. It wasn't a yes, either." *Stubborn. Sassy. Sexy. Smart.*

"Agreed. So no acceptance, but no outright rejection. In business, we call it a status quo."

"Are you suggesting you'll continue driving around until I give you an answer? Or until I give you the answer you want?" The headlights of a passing car played over her face and revealed her pursed lips.

"No, I'm telling you I want to go out with you because I want to get to know you better." Lies couched in truth worked. Truth by itself was also useful.

She sighed, impatience in the huff of breath. "I can't commit to anything right now. I can tell you I'll call, but...life is complicated."

Complicated.

A sad, provocative word that spoke volumes to whatever held back the playful woman he'd engaged on the curb in New York.

"It doesn't have to be." He faced a fork in the path but trust took time.

"And most of the time, it probably wouldn't be, but as much as I have enjoyed this and appreciated your assistance, it's time to say good-bye, Jarod." Like a lock turning, she shut him out.

"Okay." Strategic retreat and regroup time. He took the next exit and pulled into the first hotel lot he saw. "But you need sleep. You're exhausted." He put the car in park and turned in the seat to face her. "Humor me. Get a room. Get some sleep. Leave in the morning."

She arched both brows and sat forward in her seat, studying the hotel. It wasn't anything fancy, a mid-level hotel offering clean rooms, soft beds, and convenience. It was also a far cry from the five-star options she usually selected.

"Well, Louis would never look for me here." But a trace of uncertainty wavered under the words.

"No, and we'll put it on my business card. That way, if he's looking for you to use yours, we can buy you a little more time." It wasn't ideal, but if he could get her to sleep, he could move some assets around. He wanted eyes on duMonde at all times.

"You're being a little too nice to me, Mr. Parker." And she pushed him away again. The quiet determination to keep him at arm's length aggravated and enticed him.

"Nice wouldn't have an ulterior motive." He shut the car off and pocketed the keys as he stepped out. He let her chew on the bite of truth while he walked around and opened her door. She'd only put on a trace of cosmetics before leaving the plane. Her tousled curls curved around her face, and the pantsuit she wore did nothing to disguise her figure. But he missed the pajamas and ponytail.

"So you admit to having one?" she challenged, stepping out of the car, purse in hand.

"Never denied it in the first place. Getting to know you is a perk." He locked the car, leaving their bags in the backseat. "I'll bring your things to you as soon as you're tucked away in the room."

"You do realize this is my car?"

"I do." He stared back at her, unmoved by the coy twist to her expression.

"Very well," she conceded and motioned to the hotel. "I am tired."

He didn't gloat or buy she'd given up trying to shed him like a bad winter coat, but led the way inside. Booking two side-by-side rooms took less than fifteen minutes. He walked her to their rooms, checked the locks, and prowled both rooms once before leaving her to fetch the bags. Five minutes later, he handed her the room key and her briefcase from the plane.

"Try to rest. I'll see you in"— he glanced at his watch—"a few hours."

"Jarod?" She stopped him with a hand on his back before he could leave the room. He twisted to find her leaning up, standing on her tiptoes, and then her mouth brushed his. The hesitant little caress caught him off-guard, ripping the cap off his desire and dropping in a match. He slid a hand up to catch her nape, massaging her lips until her mouth opened.

Her tongue darted against his with quick, firm strokes. Her palms flattened against his chest, rubbing his shirt. Pressed against the wall, he enjoyed the teasing dance of her tongue until he caught it in a slow, lingering suck. The sensuous action drew a moan from her throat.

Yeah, this is professional. The cold, practical side of him intruded on the lazy heat consuming his good intentions. It would be so easy to pick her up, shut the door, and carry her over to the bed. If nothing else, he'd know exactly where she was while he took his time exploring the sensuous curves tormenting him.

But he couldn't afford the distraction. Not with duMonde on her scent and the Buddha close to being in his grasp. His whole body protested his mind's rationality, and he broke the kiss with far more reluctance than he'd imagined. The elusive scent of her perfume couldn't disguise the wholly feminine feel and smell of her: hot coffee and glazed donuts on a rainy morning. Decadently tempting.

"No?" she teased.

I wish. "No." He shook his head slowly, caressing the slender column of her neck with his thumb. The blouse she wore was as thin and silky as the green one from the night before. It hugged her breasts and revealed the twin peaks stabbing at the fabric. She shifted against him, sliding a hand down to his hip, teasing the erection straining against his zipper.

"Sure? We have several hours before we have to say good-bye. It's not dinner, but...."

He should be nominated for sainthood. Only years of discipline and training kept him from pinning her to the wall and stripping her naked—because really, they didn't need the bed.

"Tempting. Very tempting." He allowed himself the smallest possible pleasure and kissed the corner of her mouth and a gentle nip to her lower lip. "But I'm an old-fashioned kind of guy. I'll see you in the morning."

Her throaty chuckle went straight to his cock, and it stiffened hard enough he supposed sleep would be impossible. "You're a rare man, Jarod."

"I'll take it as a compliment. Now"— he peeled her away from him, much to his own regret, turned her around, and gave her sweet little ass a pinch—"bed."

"And pushy." She tossed the last over her shoulder, hips swaying invitingly as she walked toward the bed. "Do turn off the lights on your way out."

The little vixen was already unbuttoning her blouse. He overrode the primal need to follow and forced himself to leave. He stood outside the door, his determination wavering, but he managed the two steps to his own room and let himself in.

An icy shower.

Then phone calls.

He glanced at the wall separating their rooms. Thankfully, they didn't have an adjoining door or he might have glanced in to see her tucked into bed.

Yeah,'cause looking is what I would be doing. He walked into the bathroom and turned on the water. Emptying his pockets, he froze and checked all four again. "Son of a bitch...." Admiration and exasperation burst out. Grabbing the pair of room keys, he slid back out, but a quick look in her room found Kit Kat gone.

He ignored the elevators and jogged down the stairs. He

expected it, but he still had to check.

No car.

She'd played him.

Upstairs, he went back into her room and flipped on the light in the bathroom. A lipstick kiss decorated the center of the mirror and written below it.

Make it three to two.

He laughed. She'd tempted him and taken the keys. Smart woman.

His ego accepted the blow better than his cock. He left her room and returned to his own. The tracking device he'd planted in her purse would go active in another few hours. The chip's passive design helped it to bypass general sweeps, but if she made it more than fifty miles away, it would turn on automatically. He had assets he could activate, and he sent a message to one now, sending them to track duMonde. He couldn't go after her, yet, but he could still watch her back.

Stripping his clothes off, he ducked into the icy spray and considered his options.

Banker, my ass. Kit used her phone to GPS a route from the hotel to Hollywood. The backtracking made her teeth ache, but Jarod's persistence set off one too many warning bells. He'd dropped Louis with almost no difficulty. Granted, she froze up when Louis had his hands on her, but not Jarod. His reactions, the shrewd assessment in his gaze, the way he moved—they all spoke of a physical confidence few men possessed.

Those who did had some kind of training.

Then there was his presence on her plane. The private jet parked at gates behind several layers of airport security. He needed passkeys and clearance to travel from the public access in the airport to the private terminals. Based on the time she left the limo and when she walked out to find him aboard her plane, he had to have followed almost immediately.

Traffic thickened in the city's central areas, but she didn't experience any slowdowns. Miles had intimated her father had something to do....

Wait, I assumed Daddy did it. Miles stammered and hesitated and simply agreed with her. *Which correlates to Jarod's assertion Daddy didn't send him.*

Tapping her phone, she dialed a number and checked for her exit as it rang.

"*Buenas dias, señorita Hardwicke. ¿Como estas?*"

"*Bien, Enrique. Bien. ¿Y tu?*"

"*Asi asi.* I cannot complain. What do you need?" Enrique Tomavar worked at the British Embassy in Spain during her father's brief tenure as ambassador. He was the first man to teach her how to hide in plain sight. The British ambassador's abysmally low popularity rating meant constant threats to the family. Enrique created her first fake ID and taught her how to blend in when she didn't want to be seen. Since his resume included positions like military and government attaché, she often suspected he worked as a spy—but his affection for her remained constant.

As did his ability to fetch her in difficult times. If not for Enrique, she wouldn't have been able to get out of Morocco last year.

"I can't simply call to say hello?"

"This late, in Los Angeles? I doubt that." He always knew her location, too. Useful when she had to send him a 911—frustrating every other time.

"Fair point. I need some information about a man named Jarod Parker."

"Basic rundown, or are you looking for something more specific?" Bless him, he never asked her why.

"I want to know if he is who he says he is."

"And who does he say he is, *querida*?"

"A banker." She saw her exit and slowed to follow it.

"And you think not?"

"He took down Louis duMonde with a thumb lock in under ten seconds. I didn't even see him move. He also managed to smuggle himself aboard my private jet."

Silence, then, "Is he threatening you?"

"No. The opposite, actually. But I don't know him, and I don't think he's being honest."

More silence.

"I will find out what you need to know. Stay away until I have confirmation, *querida*."

"Already done. Don't call back. I'm going to kill the phone and dump it. I'll call you tomorrow from a burner." She had six of them in a locker, and they were easily purchased.

"Adios, cuidate."

"Adios." They rang off, and she merged into traffic on the boulevard. It took her fifteen minutes of cruising to find the right woman with the right height. She slowed and rolled down the passenger window.

The redhead leaned down to glance inside and gave her a dubious look. "Sorry, Prada. I like men."

"Perfect. I have a thousand dollars in cash and it's all yours if you don't mind swapping clothes, driving my car until 6:00 p.m. tonight, and giving someone a message for me."

"I'm sorry, what?" The woman blinked.

Thirty minutes later, Kit waved to Georgia, the woman whose clothes she'd purchased, as she drove off in the sedan. Kit had nothing on her save for one key and a paperback book. She didn't know if he'd done something to keep track of her, but his actions coupled with Louis' sudden appearance, and she didn't want to take any chances.

She walked down to the bus station and straight to a locker. Opening it, she pulled out a duffel bag and checked to make sure the lock on the bag remained in place. Slinging it over her shoulder, she walked down the concourse to the ticket window where a sleepy man flipped through a magazine.

"Do you have any coaches leaving for Half Moon Bay today?" She chewed gum, which distracted from her accent, and kept the black hat low over her eyes. She had tucked all of her red hair underneath it. The tank top and skinny jeans were thankfully nondescript, and she could buy some comfortable shoes. She'd miss the Jimmy Choos she gave to Georgia.

The man sat forward and tapped some info into his computer. "Coach leaves at seven. Sixty-eight seventy-five, round-trip."

"Perfect." She counted out the cash, mostly in tens, fives, and singles. Never be without cash, Enrique told her. She could leave cash stores in various places, so if she needed to slip away unnoticed, she wouldn't leave a trace with her credit cards or private security. Secondly, keep the cash in low denominations. It made most people impatient to wait for someone to count it out, and then they paid attention to other things. Nothing zeroed a retail or transportation clerk in more than crisp fifty and one hundred-dollar bills.

She made sure to wash and dry any new money she took out of the bank to give it a rumpled, ill-used appearance. She handed him sixty-nine dollars and got a quarter and her ticket back.

"Have a nice trip." But the clerk had already returned to his magazine.

She checked the bus number and her watch, after four-thirty. She left the terminal and walked around the corner to a coffee shop. Sliding into a seat in the back, she wedged the duffel bag between her and the wall. Propping her feet on the opposite bench, she pulled out the book.

"What can I get ya?" a woman on the sad side of her forties with tired eyes and an even worse dye job asked.

"Coffee, please." She resisted the urge to spit out her gum. Soon enough for that when she didn't have to talk and could drink her coffee instead. "And bacon and eggs—eggs over hard, bacon crisp, and, if you have them, hash browns extra crispy."

"Toast?" The waitress wrote it down.

"Hmm—whole wheat with some jam as well."

"You got it."

Kit didn't have to worry about the waitress paying attention to her; the woman's gaze skipped twice to her watch in the time she wrote down the order. She wanted to go home, which meant she'd deliver the food and coffee and leave her be.

Glancing at her watch, Kit flipped the book open to the dog-eared page and settled in to wait for her bus.

But the words blurred against the page. *Jarod isn't a banker.* She'd never seen him before the meeting, and he was right about one thing—she did notice people. She knew every employee she'd ever met, on sight if not by name. She could always tell when she'd met someone before and didn't recognize them—the spark in their eyes, the friendly surprise and ease in their expressions. She knew and reacted accordingly.

He demonstrated none of those qualities.

But he knew me. I wasn't such great a mystery to him...and he appeared really worried about what Miles told me on the phone.

So either he ran a con on Miles....

Or he found out about the Raphael. The Raphael she'd seen in Miles' collection six months before and knew didn't belong there. At the time, she'd said nothing. After all, it took a thief to know a thief.

And she was an exceptionally talented thief.

This is all supposition. Maybe he saw me as a potential bankroll for his business efforts. The thought didn't live very long because he sure as hell didn't kiss like he wanted her money.

He wanted her.

The waitress returned with the coffee and breakfast. She added some sugar and cream to her cup and stirred it. Maybe she owed Jarod the benefit of the doubt. He could like her. She wasn't an unattractive a woman. His reasons for following the plane, for getting on board—hell, even his actions at the airport could all have a plausible explanation.

Or he could just want the Buddha—like everyone else.

A shiver raced up her spine, and, she wasn't afraid to admit, a wave of disappointment followed. If all Jarod wanted was the artifact, he would be sorely disappointed. Her appetite waned at the thought. The door opened at the front of the diner. She watched a couple of construction workers pad in, yawning. They took seats at the front counter.

She cut into her eggs and ignored the doubts niggling in the back of her mind. She had forty-eight hours to finish this, and then it would be over and done with. Years of hunting, globe hopping, and flirting with danger and she could finally put the entire matter of *The Fortunate Buddha* to rest.

Focusing on the light at the end of the tunnel, and not the fact she already missed Jarod's company, helped her finish her breakfast. She watched the door every time it opened. She didn't need Jarod or Louis finding her right now. Once she boarded the bus, she'd disappear.

This was what she wanted. Unfortunately, every time the door did open and it wasn't Jarod, her stomach sank.

Stop it. She picked up the book and forced herself to read. At least the seventeenth century spy novel's heroine got to sleep with the man she stole her information from—all well and good until he found out what she was up to and then the chase ensued.

He'd caught up to the dangerous duchess, and it didn't take much to imagine these two in the throes of angry sex. *I wonder if Jarod thinks hot sex is what he'll get when he catches up to Georgia.*

The image of his face when he discovered her ruse made her smile.

Chapter Five

The moment the redhead exited the sedan and sashayed into the coffee shop, he knew she wasn't Kit. Biting back a curse, Jarod backed his car into a parking space, locked it up, and followed the woman inside. She stood at the counter, ordering a triple foam nightmare creation. From a distance, the color of her hair seemed similar, but, up close, looked too brassy. The way she moved, hard and jerky, appearing too defensive, didn't fit Kit either. She stalked forward as though hoping to intimidate others into leaving her alone, all brash and flash without the natural sensuality or smooth seduction.

He'd traced the wrong woman. Slipping back outside, he checked the car. Kit's. Her bag and purse sat on the passenger seat in bold statement. Checking his phone, the GPS told him he was right on top of the tracker. Thumbing it off, he slid the phone into his pocket and leaned back against the car to wait.

The redhead emerged with a tall cup in her hand. She saw him immediately. Her relaxed expression stiffened, becoming almost predatory. He stared at her as she strode toward him. "You must be Jarod."

Surprise flared in his gut, like a match being struck against wood, burning away doubt. "And you are?"

"I'm Georgia." She grinned. The faint yellowing of her teeth didn't detract from the warmth the expression added to her face.

"Good evening, Georgia." He infused the words with a patience he didn't really feel. "This isn't your car, is it?"

"Well, not exactly. But, I do have a slip signed over to me and legal permission to drive it for as long as I wish." She took a long swallow of coffee. The lines around her eyes were tight with worry, and, despite the friendly curve of her lips, the corners of her mouth seemed strained.

"Well, if I were to call the police...."

"Look, I don't want any trouble. You're Jarod, so I can answer your questions. If you were the other guy, I wouldn't have even come back out of the coffee shop."

The other guy. duMonde? His eyes narrowed as she juggled her coffee cup and reached into her purse to pull out—Kit's cell phone. He recognized the case. Hell, he recognized her whole ensemble. Georgia wore a two thousand dollar pantsuit and four thousand dollar shoes. She thumbed the screen on and flipped from text messages to photos and held it up.

"See, this is you." Clearly a photo of him sitting across from Kit on the plane. When did the little vixen snap the shot? "And this is the other guy."

The other, indeed duMonde, but the photo came from a distance and looked saved from the Internet.

"All right, so you can talk to me. Talk."

"First, let me say I am only the messenger. She promised me you wouldn't shoot me for saying this."

The corner of his mouth turned up. "She's right. I won't."

"She said to tell you, 'Make it three to three, now we're tied.'" Georgia punctuated the sentence with a pair of kissing sounds.

His eyebrows climbed.

"Hey, the kisses were from her. She made me repeat it four times, until I had it down."

A headache gathered in the back of his skull. "When did she do this?"

Georgia swallowed another mouthful of coffee before answering. "Last night. She cruised the boulevard. Took her for a high roller. They like to slum it, sometimes. Course, I don't do chicks." She gave him the once over, and he ignored the speculative invitation in her eyes. "Anyway, she offered me a grand—cash—and all I had to do was swap clothes and drive her car around until at least 6:00 p.m. tonight. She told me there were two men who might be looking for her. You were okay, but I should avoid the other guy at all costs."

The pain in his head began to hammer. Twice, he'd underestimated Lady Hardwicke's resourcefulness. He wouldn't make the same mistake again. "And that's it?"

"Pretty much. She gave me her phone, and there's a digital tablet in the car and some files." She shrugged. "She waved me off, and it was the last I saw of her." She closed her eyes a half second and glanced down during her answer.

"Really?" He didn't know her well enough to assume the deflection a lie, but the guilt trailing through her gaze told him to hang onto this thread.

"Okay, maybe I circled the block a couple of times to make sure she wasn't screwing me over."

"She just gave you a thousand dollars in cash. She didn't have time to screw you over." And Georgia was only a pawn in the game. No need to sacrifice her or make her task unnecessarily hard.

The woman flushed a faint shade of crimson, and guilt worried the lines around her mouth. "True. But it's one hell of an expensive car and a lot of cash. No one's that nice just to ask you to drive around and not be up to no good. So...maybe I watched where she went, and maybe I made sure there wasn't a body in the trunk before I hit a freeway."

He didn't smile, but he couldn't fault her logic. "So, where did she go?"

"Bus station. Crazy chick. She has all kinds of cash and this car, and she heads to the bus station? Why would anyone go there?"

Because a bus had less security, and no one would look for the heiress to the Hardwicke fortunes aboard one. Jarod pulled a hundred out of his wallet and handed it to her. "I want her things from the car."

"Hey, all yours. Do you want the car?" Concern and uncertainty flickered in her expression.

"Nope. You can keep it." He waited for the telltale beep indicating she'd unlocked it then grabbed the bags and jacket. "And I need her phone."

If Louis tracked her with any of this.... He paused and studied the car. "Tell you what. Take the car to 44th and Lex downtown, talk to Mitch. Tell him you need an exterminator. He'll take care of cleaning the car."

Georgia's eyes rounded, and she blinked at him owlishly. "Is there something wrong with my car?"

The proprietary note in her voice amused him. "Probably not, but it never hurts." He handed her another hundred. "Consider it on me."

She traded the phone for the hundred, and he carried all of it with him. He hoped Georgia listened, because Louis had time to put a tracking device on the car since he'd arrived at the airport first—but his arrival as soon as they departed suggested he'd *only* made it himself. Dropping her gear on the passenger seat, Jarod started his own car and kept an eye on Georgia. He sorted through everything in the bag—files, her digital tablet, a change of clothes, and a slim pack of tampons. Nothing to go on.

Her purse revealed even less. Her wallet was there, but she'd stripped the credit cards' magnetic stripes. No I.D. card or passport—she either took them with her, left them on her plane, or maybe Georgia helped herself. He dismissed the last. Kit Kat had planned to go into the wind the minute she arrived in Los Angeles. But...she'd taken the time to fly to L.A.

So why Los Angeles? The bus he understood. But had she planned to use a bus from the beginning? No—the car.

Georgia talked on her own cell phone now, sitting in the car across from him. She hadn't backed out of her parking space. The car had waited in the private hanger for Kit's arrival. She'd planned to drive away from her plane, her security, and any other observers, in all likelihood, to another destination to pick up another car.

His phone rang. He recognized the number, so he hit the answer button. "Yes?"

"I'm at the Malibu estate. She's not here. She hasn't been here in some time. One of the field workers said she rarely stays at the estate even when she is in town, though."

"Did he say why?"

"No, he mentioned she attended parties and social functions at the estate, but they always saw her leave as soon as the parties ended and she didn't always return. His sister is one of the house maids, and Lady Hardwicke's things are often packed by them and sent to the airport to be picked up by her plane."

"How often does she visit?"

"One moment." The voices on the other end of the phone muffled as though the caller covered the phone to ask a question. Jarod continued to study Kit's vehicle while he waited. "Three to four times a year since age sixteen. Get this—her father threw a huge soiree here at the estate on her sixteenth birthday, but the guest of honor never made an appearance. The rumor here is she ran away...but a couple of weeks later, she returned, and everyone acted like nothing happened. Since then, she visits regularly but never stays."

"See if you can find out anything more about that summer."

"You got it."

The man rang off, and Jarod started his car. Georgia backed out of her parking spot and waved as she drove off. He shook his head. He needed to head to the Hollywood bus terminal and review what, if any, security tapes they had. Which meant another call and another favor.

His Kit Kat became increasingly expensive.

Two hours later, he stared at three monitors. The Greyhound station had upgraded their surveillance since 9/11, but the angles were shit. He knew what time Kit met with Georgia on the boulevard, so he narrowed his search window to those two hours. How many people bought tickets or passed through the station at four in the morning?

Too many.

"Stop." The tech hit the space bar at his word, and all three images froze. "Back camera three up ten seconds."

The man complied. A leggy woman in skinny jeans and a red tank top sauntered across in slow motion. A black cap hid her hair, but he didn't need to see it. She moved with absolute confidence and control. "Follow her." He pointed to the screen.

The man nodded and started typing. The screens shifted. She walked from camera three onto four and then around the corner onto seven. At a locker, she inserted a key and pulled out a duffel bag. She opened it but blocked their view of the contents.

Leaving the locker, she followed a path which took her out of sight until they found her on camera six, four, and back to three. She disappeared again, for ten seconds, before appearing on camera one at the ticket window.

She paid cash.

Jarod had to admire her skill.

She was good.

"Can you tell me her destination?"

The third man in the booth, the station manager, nodded. "Give me a minute." He swiveled to face another computer terminal and typed in some information.

"She left here," the guard scrolling the tapes said. "Right after she bought the ticket, she exited the station...maybe the buy was a distraction?"

Maybe. Jarod waited for the manager.

"Seven a.m. departure for Half Moon Bay. It's about seven hours north of here."

"Run it forward." Jarod glanced back at the screens, but the guard was already doing it. She appeared in the station at six fifty-five. They followed her route to the departure lanes, and, sure enough, she and her duffel bag boarded the bus. She didn't give the duffel to the driver for storage, waving him off with a quick smile.

The bus left at seven in the morning, and it was after five now. She was in Half Moon Bay. "Call ahead to the bus station. Send them this photo and see if she boarded another bus."

The manager nodded. "Should we warn the driver? I know she's already left the one she booked on, but if she's a credible threat...."

Jarod shook his head once. "No. I'll take care of this, and I don't want her knowing anyone is coming." He relied on the call from his contact at Homeland Security to keep these guys in line. They'd been more than cooperative.

Pulling out his phone, he sent another text. He didn't have a single asset in the area, but he could put researchers on trying to link Kit with Half Moon Bay. The small seaside town didn't offer any direct clues. He couldn't discount the possibility of false trails. The resourceful and intelligent woman knew someone hunted her.

"Do me a favor." He leaned back down to the guard. "Can you tell if a bus is coming in from Half Moon Bay today?"

"It's probably a round-trip service." The guard nodded, switching his screen to the scheduler. He typed in the bus number. "And it's due back here at eight fifteen."

"Does the bus have a camera on board?"

The guard blinked. "Yeah, but we're not supposed to—"

"Humor me. I'll look away. Just tell me if she's there."

"Why would she be?"

"Humor me," Jarod repeated.

The guard glanced over his shoulder toward the manager, and the man gave him an impatient nod, continuing to talk to the Half Moon Bay station. The guard glanced up at Jarod, and he made a point of turning away from the screens but watched instead via the overhead mirror. The man typed in a password, accessed a system and a stop motion feed came in from the bus. Several passengers were dozing in the dark. But each strike of the spacebar brought another section into focus.

"I don't see her." The guard actually sounded relieved.

But Jarod did see her. She'd changed clothes, added a pair of reading glasses and a green baseball cap rather than black. She sat three feet from the driver with the duffel bag on the seat next to her.

"Thanks." He glanced at his watch. He had three hours before she arrived. "Does it make any more stops before it gets here?"

"Nope. Sorry she's not there."

The manager hung up the phone. "She arrived. They tracked her leaving the terminal. She didn't board any other buses."

"Thank you for your help, gentlemen." He let the men off the hook and headed out. She'd set a false trail to Half Moon Bay, but if she maintained a locker at this bus terminal, she might have others along the route. He sent orders to an asset in San Francisco to drive there and check it out. He had time to change before she arrived back in Los Angeles.

Four to three, sweetheart.

Her ass ached by the time she descended the steps from the bus. The round-trip took her off the grid for most of the day, and if they did trace her path, they'd have trouble pinpointing her. She knew how to change her appearance so even if the security guards saw her, they'd see a college student or maybe an aspiring actress fresh off the farm. It didn't really matter as long as they didn't see Lady Katherine Hardwicke.

Duffel bag slung over her shoulder, she blended in with the shuffling crowd weaving through the terminal. Several diverted to the bathrooms, and still more raced out to the front to light up a cigarette. She gave the blue haze of nicotine addiction a wide berth and turned right to head up the boulevard.

She wanted food, a shower, and ten hours of sleep, not necessarily in that order. It was late on Saturday. She couldn't pick up the keys she needed until lunchtime on Sunday. It would be Monday before she could drive to Bakersfield.

The ticking clock seemed to beat with every pulse of her heart. But she couldn't move any faster. If she'd rushed to pick it up today with Louis and Jarod breathing down her neck, it would have cost her more time than the bus trip. Playing it cool and safe were her only options. She glanced at the watch on her wrist, almost nine. She didn't want to stop anywhere for food, so she would order room service.

Twisting to walk backwards, she lifted a hand and hailed a passing taxi three blocks from the bus station. The yellow cab swung in, and she opened the back door and slid in with her duffel. "The Westin Pasadena, please."

"You got it." The driver pulled back out into traffic with barely a glance at her.

Kit wrapped her fist around the duffel bag straps and stared out the window. The nightlife hopped on the boulevard, throngs of tourists thicker in some spots than others. She loved these types of churning city centers where a person could easily get lost amongst a sea of strangers. Three turns later, the taxi surged onto one of the dozen arteries serving the greater Los Angeles area. The drive from Hollywood to Pasadena would cost, but she had enough cash in the bag to take care of expenses through the weekend.

Thirty-five minutes later, a yawn splitting her jaw, she gave the driver an extra twenty for a tip and entered the hotel lobby. It took her fifteen minutes to get a room. She paid cash and used one of the three IDs hidden in the duffel. Tara Pelfrey would be burned after the trip, but she didn't care.

"Can you go ahead and place an order with room service for me?" She went for charm with the clerk. The man assured her he could, so she asked for a shrimp and lobster pasta with water and a pot of coffee. She didn't really need the caffeine, but she craved it.

The tenth floor room boasted one king-size bed, a forty-inch television screen, and a view of Los Angeles. She ignored all three and stripped to get in the shower. Washing away a day's worth of sweat and bus smells went a long way toward restoring her mood. She wrapped a towel around her head and another around her body before sacking up the second set of clothes she would abandon. She'd left Georgia's in a trash bin in Half Moon Bay. The shorts and *I heart L.A.* T-shirt in her bag would take care of tomorrow, and she could shop for anything else she needed.

Shoving the plastic bag of discarded clothes into the trashcan, she padded back to the closet. The Westin always provided robes. She'd barely tugged it from the hanger before someone knocked on the door. "Room service," they called through.

"One moment." She slipped on the robe and glanced through

the peephole. A white shirt, black tie, and large tray filled her line of sight. Opening the door, she pulled it wide and pointed to the desk. "If you wouldn't mind...."

"Not at all." The waiter carried the tray in and set it down. She pulled the towel off her head and rubbed at her damp hair while he took the silver lids off the plates. Reaching into the bathroom, she pulled a ten off the stack of bills she had left and turned back to find the waiter standing between her and the door.

Every hair on her body stood up as she met the knowing brown eyes.

"Jarod."

"Kit Kat."

How the hell...?

Her gut churned. She mentally catalogued the room. Tenth floor. The balcony looked out over the city and the parking lot, not a pool. Jarod stood between her and the only other viable exit. He didn't appear to be armed. She had a Taser in the bag, but not in direct reach.

Like a Mexican standoff, they stared at each other. She couldn't process how the hell he'd found her. Her limited options narrowed down to fight, seduce, or surrender.

She wasn't ready for any of them. "You're not a banker."

"No," he agreed. "I'm not. Go sit down...and eat. You look tired."

"Who are you?"

"I could ask you the same question." He blew out a breath and held up a hand. "Go eat, Kit Kat, before you fall down. We can talk about everything when we're done."

She lifted her chin. She was not giving up. She had not come this far, worked this hard, to lose now. "You need to go."

"After we talk." He nodded again, very agreeable. But she recognized the tone. She used it all the time. Placate the upset one and do whatever after they calmed down.

"I could scream." The warning didn't seem to have any effect on him. If anything, the sensuous curve of his mouth turned up into a wolfish grin.

"You could. But if you were going to do it, you would have screamed already. I give you my word, I'm not here to hurt you."

"Then get out. Walk out the door right now."

"No."

Her heart slammed against the cage of her ribs, beating faster than a mad hummingbird, desperate for escape. Time to switch tactics. She took a step toward him and forced her shoulders to relax. "Jarod."

"If you try to kiss me again, I'll spank you. Now go eat." He probably meant to sound intimidating, but damn if his order didn't turn her on. Liquid heat rolled through her blood, and she sucked in a breath.

"You liked it when I kissed you." Defiance reared up inside her, crushing the spike of fear.

"Didn't say otherwise. But you and I, we need to talk. First, however, you need to eat before you pass out."

"I never pass out." She denied the lightheaded sensation sweeping over her.

Jarod took her arm and tugged her gently over to the desk. He pulled out the chair and gave her a nudge until she sat. She expected him to be angry and—from the muscle ticking in his jaw—he probably was. But his touch gave nothing away. He retreated a couple of steps and perched on the edge of the bed.

"Eat," he repeated. "Please."

The please did it. She fell back into the chair and stared at him. "Why are you following me, Jarod?"

"If I promise to give you the truth when you're done, will you eat? You're pale, and your eyes are glassy, and I think you're in shock. Eat. Drink some of the coffee. Get your blood sugar up, and then we can talk." The brisk orders dissolved in the request, and she pulled her gaze away from him to look at the food.

"I don't get how you found me here...." She'd done everything the way she'd learned. No one ever followed her before—in fact, the only person she'd talked to aside from the night clerk was the....

She froze and flicked a look up at him.

He spread his hands wide. "You got it."

He was the taxi driver.

He waited for her outside the bus terminal.

He knew she'd be coming back.

"Who are you?" Her fingers trembled as she wrapped them around the fork.

He didn't look away from her. "I'm your friend, and I can help you."

"With?" The tension stretched her nerves to the breaking point.

Clasping his hands together, he leaned forward, elbows on his knees. "*The Fortunate Buddha.*"

And the last shred of her hope snapped. Stabbing the fork into a piece of lobster, she forced a smile past the anxiety. "The what?"

"No more games, Kit Kat. This is serious. duMonde is working his way through Los Angeles, looking for you."

She let his warning roll off her back. "Well, I hope he can learn to live with disappointment."

"If I can find you, so can he."

"Then I'll get a restraining order." Maybe she could still play this off. "It doesn't matter. He doesn't know where I am right now, and I'll be leaving tomorrow. I can stay ahead of him."

"Can you?" Jarod's expression didn't change.

"I outran you, didn't I?"

"True. And yet, here I am.... Oh, and the score is four to three. Thank you for the wild goose chase. I enjoyed it."

Laughter bounced up inside her, and she took another bite. "Apparently not well enough to remain distracted by it."

"Chasing you is nowhere near as interesting as catching you."

The liquid heat his earlier order stirred flamed hotter. She shifted in the chair, all too aware of her nudity beneath the robe. She enjoyed the game, the hunt, and the chase. But she couldn't afford to let him catch her...not yet.

"You haven't caught me yet." She licked her lips, her gaze colliding with his. A mistake because the wild want in his gaze couldn't be mistaken for anything else.

"I know," he murmured, his voice a seductive caress.

Her stomach flip-flopped, and she couldn't suppress the shudder of reaction. "What if I don't want to be caught?"

He didn't touch her. He didn't reach out. He didn't move. He simply stared at her. "What do you want?"

You. The unbidden response burst through her mind, and she pushed the plate and fork away. She must be exhausted because her mind filled with images of the two of them, kissing, touching, caressing, and tumbling back onto the bed.

But she couldn't afford to chase such a prize...not now.

"Two days." She swallowed. "I want two days."

He canted his head to the right and lifted his brows. "And then?"

"Nothing. And then nothing. You asked me what I wanted...I want two days. I need it." Her pulse continued to rabbit, and she let her gaze drift to the bed. She could sleep with him—hell, she wanted to—and then, while he slept, she could get the hell out of here.

"Eat your dinner and I'll give you two days."

She blinked slowly. "I'm sorry, what?"

"You heard me." He stood and walked over to the phone. Hitting the button for room service, he waited for the other end to be answered. "Yes, could you send up another plate of the shrimp and lobster pasta, fresh coffee, and some bread? Yes. Yes. Thank you."

He hung up then crossed to the door. He flipped the security latch, stripped off his jacket, and hung it up.

"What are you doing?"

"I'm showing you good faith and letting you begin your two days." He watched her from his station by the door, his expression unreadable. "Eat."

She opened her mouth to protest but thought better of it. She needed two days. He gave her some time. They needed to talk, but...he had to sleep sometime. Regulating her breathing, she dug into her meal.

"And, Kit Kat?"

"Yes?" She ate another mouthful.

"If you run again...all bets are off."

We'll see. She sighed, the food already helped.

Chapter Six

H er posture, curled onto her side away from him, might appear relaxed, but he didn't fool himself into thinking she'd gone to sleep. They'd eaten their meals in respective silence. Jarod could almost hear the wheels whirring in her mind as she considered her options.

Feigning sleep provided her with the best option to continue plotting what she would do when he drifted off. Unfortunately for her, he could maintain wakefulness for up to eighty-six hours with only the lightest of dozes. He'd dimmed the lights when she lay down, but the screen on his phone allowed him to continue his work.

Louis duMonde was out of custody and checked into the Avalon in Beverly Hills. In addition to the two men at the airport, four more had arrived in the last three hours. Jarod told the asset to stay in place and requested a second for back up. If he needed more, then he needed to request them ASAP. He did not want duMonde slipping his leash.

"You're not going to go to sleep, are you?" The quiet question drifted across the room, and he glanced over. She rolled onto her right side and propped her head up. She'd gotten back most of her color and a great deal of her spirit. His arrival had scared the hell out of her, but he ignored the twinge of regret at the blank look in her eyes—and the way all the color drained from her face.

"Not likely, no. But you should."

"I can't." The dim glow of his phone left most of her face in shadow.

"Why not?"

"I dozed on the bus today—too much, I guess. I'm tired, but I can't sleep."

When he thumbed his phone off, the room plunged into darkness without the blue glow. "Try regulating your breathing."

Her laughter teased his ears, like a whispered caress across his senses. "I've tried. I think it might be the presence of an uninvited visitor in my hotel room."

"If you'd stayed in the first room I set up for you, you could have slept by yourself." The near involuntary curving of his lips made him glad for the darkness.

"Who are you, Jarod Parker?"

"A man doing his job."

She snorted. "I won't insult your intelligence if you won't insult mine."

"All right." If she wanted to talk about it now, they would. "I'm a recovery agent. I'm here to pick up *The Fortunate Buddha*."

"And what is *The Fortunate Buddha*?" Amusement hummed under the words.

"What's that about not insulting my intelligence?" He leaned back in the chair, extending his legs out in front of him. Tucking the phone in his pocket, he focused on staying in the chair and not walking over to stretch out on the bed next to her.

"I'm not insulting your intelligence. You accused me of having it—"

"Which you do."

"I didn't say I did." She argued, but the playfulness in her words didn't waver.

"You didn't protest the accusation either."

"Innocent people don't have to protest. That's some really flimsy logic if you're going to accuse me of being in possession of a stolen item."

"You went out of your way to sneak off. You have a viscount with a known habit for the acquisition of stolen goods hunting you. But those are only two of the current facts. You were also in Geneva, Switzerland, when it went missing from the same viscount's safe. You left a note for the agent assigned to retrieve it along with a digital recording of her in Morocco. You were in New York when the Buddha was retrieved from the Museum by the NYPD and shortly before it disappeared from their evidence lock up." He ticked off the events one after another on his fingers.

"Circumstantial at best." Satisfaction colored her answer.

Amusement surged through him. She was absolutely right. The circumstantial evidence wouldn't earn a search warrant, but he didn't need a warrant. "And you still haven't denied it."

"Do you want me to deny it?" The swishing noise of the sheets told him she moved. He looked away from the side of the bed a moment before the light snapped on. She sat up in the bed, a pillow in her lap and her knees up. Her green-eyed gaze met his with frank determination. She appeared almost fragile, but possessed a tough, resourceful streak.

"No." He shook his head once. "I want to help you."

She blinked. "I'm sorry, what?"

"You heard me." He tipped his head to the side. He enjoyed watching her mind at work and physical cues like the narrowing of her eyes, chewing the inside of her cheek, or the flexing of her fingers against the pillow.

"If I already took it—which, according to you, I did—why do I need help?" She didn't avoid his gaze or play coy. Another mark in her favor, the direct intelligence and courage shimmering in those eyes was far more attractive than her considerable beauty.

"What would you have done if I hadn't been there at the airport?"

"The captain and co-pilot would have helped, and I wouldn't have left the plane before they cleared the area." The too swift answer wasn't disingenuous, but she shook her head. "But I am glad you were there."

And the wall between them developed the first real fissure. So he applied pressure to it. "Why?"

"Because Viscount duMonde"—she sighed and pushed the pillow away while sliding off the bed—"is not a nice man. He's spoiled, arrogant, and known to be rather violent at times." She'd gone to bed in a T-shirt, and it hit the middle of her thighs like an invitation for exploration. He kept his gaze on her face, even if the rest of his body hummed to awareness.

"Then we are agreed on him."

"I suppose. Is there any coffee left?" She glanced at the tray, and he stood to reach for the barely warm carafe.

"There is, but let me order us some more."

"Okay." She circled around him and walked to the sliding door. He dialed room service as she unlatched it and let in the cool night air. She didn't walk out onto the balcony, choosing to lean on the doorframe and study the city beyond.

The shirt curved up her hip as she folded her arms, revealing gorgeous bare thigh. Letting out a slow breath, he ordered the coffee and hung up. Probably better to stay on this side of the room anyway. He leaned back against the wall.

"You said I could have a couple of days. Are you planning to arrest me?"

"As you said, I only have circumstantial evidence." He could pull strings and have her detained, but no matter how many times he entertained the idea, he dismissed it.

She lapsed into silence, and he let her continue to work the Gordian knot of her situation out in her mind. When the coffee arrived, he checked the peephole first and didn't let their waiter in, taking the tray himself and relocking the door. Kit remained in the doorframe while he set up the coffee and poured two fresh mugs.

"So, you're not a banker," she said when he handed her the cup.

"No." He nodded.

"And you're not law enforcement."

He smiled and took a sip. "No."

"I didn't think so. Even Interpol needs more than circumstantial to push their way into someone's life and take them hostage."

"Do you feel like a hostage?" He frowned.

Shrugging, she walked out onto the balcony and leaned against the rail, coffee mug cradled in her hand. The breeze carried the barest hints of moisture, as if it rained somewhere else. "Somewhat."

"You're not a hostage."

"So I can grab my things and walk out the door?" Skepticism spread thickly across the top of the question.

"Absolutely. But I'll go with you."

"I don't need a keeper."

"Maybe. But duMonde isn't in custody anymore. He's also got more men in the city."

Her mouth tightened, and he regretted having to scare her, but the independent streak in her could get her killed. "How do you know?"

"Because I'm having him watched. I'll know when he moves and where he goes. But all he has to do is pick up a phone and call in someone I don't see and you'll have another bloodhound on your trail." Were he in duMonde's position, he would make the same decision. In fact, he'd have a dozen boots on the ground, combing the city for the target.

"He has no idea where I am. You wouldn't have known if you hadn't been a cab driver, and how did you do it? You didn't look like you in the cab."

It was his turn to be startled, but he covered it up with another swallow of the coffee. "I know how to blend in...a skill you obviously picked up somewhere."

"A skill I've needed over the years. My father is a very influential man, and his position earns me a lot of unwanted and unwarranted attention. What's your excuse?" Her eyes blazed with renewed temper and challenge. He preferred this woman, cunning, clever, and creative to the worried, almost desperate tone of the one courting defeat moments earlier.

"My work requires anonymity more often than not. So I've learned how to blend in when needed." A breeze pushed at her tousled curls, and he itched to tuck an errant strand behind her ear.

"Who do you work for?"

He'd debated how to answer since deciding on the direct approach. Perhaps one thing to infiltrate her business meeting and even hitch a ride on her plane, but coming to her hotel room and attaching himself to her hip meant the same rope he would use to control her kept him tied to her.

How much truth did he give her? How much did he dare?

"Do you have the Buddha?" He turned the question back on her in a calculated gamble.

"What does it have to do with who you work for?" She called his bluff.

"Everything. But let's set the issue aside for the moment." They needed to change tactics, and he needed her to trust him.

"Why?" She wasn't as willing as he to let it go.

"Because the immediate threat is to you personally. Let's say you have the Buddha." He held up a hand, stifling her objection. "For the moment, let's allege you have *The Fortunate Buddha* in your possession. Louis duMonde has a vested interest in the item. Stolen from him in Geneva, he wants it returned to him, and he thinks you have it."

"And did you have anything to do with why he thinks I do?"

He shook his head. He wasn't even entirely sure Louis did think Kit had the Buddha, but it was the only plausible reason the man would be bringing in reinforcements and why he'd followed her to California. None of their research turned up a romantic or personal connection between Lady Hardwicke and the viscount, so his interest had to be business.

The Fortunate Buddha business.

"I only have your word for it."

"True, and I only have your word you don't have the Buddha in your duffel in the room right now."

Her nostrils flared with the swift intake of breath, and her mouth tightened. He'd poked her temper and her honor in one coordinated verbal attack. She spun on a heel and marched into the hotel room. Putting her coffee cup on the dresser, she bent down, and every thought in his head bled down to his groin.

A pair of sheer lace panties hugged her very round bottom. The nude color blended with her skin tone and, if not for the delicate pattern, he'd have thought her nude from the waist down. A hint of red hidden behind the scrap of lace, answering an internal question he'd been trying not to think about.

The flame-haired vixen was a very natural redhead.

Very.

She stood up abruptly and flung the duffel bag at him. It bounced off his chest, but he caught it before it fell to floor. All the moisture left his mouth because the heat in her eyes and the flush warming her cheeks gave him more ideas.

Ideas he didn't need her bag for.

"Well, look." She motioned to the bag, one hand on her hip and the other reaching up to shove through the curls falling into her face. Rumpled, warm, and adorable. He'd kill duMonde before he let him get his hands on her again.

"What?" she demanded when he continued to stare at her.

"You're beautiful." He breathed out on the compliment. "Really beautiful."

Her mouth opened and then snapped shut again, as though she wasn't sure what to say. She moistened her lips. "Thank you. But what does my appearance have to do with searching the bag?"

"Not a damn thing." He set the bag on the chair and the coffee cup on the table.

"You're not going to search it? You have my permission." Her chin came up, but the challenge in her expression turned wary.

He shook his head and walked toward her. The light glimmered off the dampness on her lower—exceptionally kissable—lip. "No."

She retreated, but he pressed forward, undeterred. Her perfume reminded him of marzipan, sweet and decadent. When she backed up against the dresser, he reached out and brushed one finger down the curve of her cheek to trace the outline of her lips.

"What are you doing?" Her breath whispered across his fingertip.

"Would you prefer an explanation?" He lifted his brows. "Or an invitation?"

Her throat tightened with a swallow, and her breath came in faster, shallow puffs. It warmed his skin. "You said you didn't want to kiss me."

"No, I didn't." Leaning closer, he traced the line of her face to the curl insisting on falling into her eyes. He wound it around his finger then tugged it back to tuck behind her ear. "I said, if you kissed me again, I'd spank you."

The corners of her mouth quirked. "That's almost the same thing."

He shook his head slowly. "It's not the same thing at all."

She pressed a hand to his chest. "I don't know you."

"I know." He closed the gap until his lips were mere millimeters from hers. "Do you want me to kiss you?"

"If I say no?" The tip of her nose brushed his, the breathy little words adding a wave of fresh torment to his already hypersensitive libido.

"Then we can talk about the item you didn't steal some more and why you need two—"

Her mouth fused to his, silencing him. The rational portion of his mind struggled to hang onto the logical result of this kiss, but he shut it off and enjoyed the feel of satin and heat where their breath mingled and her tongue stroked along his. Her arms twined around his neck, and he gave into the indulgent desire to cup her lace-covered bottom. All soft curves and dizzying sensation, he drank from the kiss like a man dying of thirst.

He had a hundred reasons to end the kiss immediately. His cock strained against his pants, as hard and stiff as a high school senior on his first date. She was the prime suspect in a globe-spanning criminal endeavor. She possessed a priceless artifact he needed to return. So many reasons to stop, and he needed only one to scoop her up in his arms and devour the sweet, tart flavor of her mouth.

He wanted her.

Her nails dug into his shirt, and she pulled him closer. The soft hum of her moan vibrated through him, and he lifted her up until her thighs locked on his hips and her ankles crossed behind his legs. The T-shirt rode up, and he followed the line of her spine. Exactly as soft as he imagined it would be.

Twisting away from the dresser, he carried her to the bed and followed her down onto the rumpled sheets. Weight braced on one hand, he let his fingers explore the soft skin around her belly button before tracing a path up to cup one breast. She gasped and pulled away from the kiss, panting. He massaged her breast gently, all too aware of the burgeoning stiffness in her nipple.

He nuzzled the corner of her mouth. Her eyes darkened as he rolled her nipple between his thumb and forefinger. "Truce?"

"So we can have sex?" She laughed. "Where's the fun in that?"

Dipping his head down, he caught the other nipple through her T-shirt and drew it against his teeth, and she arched her back. Her hands latched onto his hair, and he drummed the turgid peak with his tongue until the shirt shaped it perfectly, clinging to the pebbled bud.

He shifted to his side and traced his fingers over her belly, abandoning the breast he very much wanted to continue tormenting. "This is a bad idea."

Kit sighed and closed her eyes. "Yes, it is."

Running his hand up and down the hourglass line from her ribs to her hips, he struggled to bring his mind back to the task. Every time his fingers brushed over the waistband of her panties, he wanted to go further. He slid one fingertip beneath the hem and stroked the skin beneath it.

"You're not stopping." She trailed one hand against his scalp, tingles radiating out from every stroke of her nails.

"I know. I'm considering the possible ways this ends." He flattened his palm against her abdomen and glided the heel of his hand down to the soft curls between her legs. Her sharp inhale pushed her breasts up, and he caught the damp tip through the fabric. Her foot slid up the bed, her legs parting farther, and the internal war slid further in favor of the one reason to say the hell with it. He hadn't found a woman this responsive or this enticing in years.

He could keep the two separate.

"Maybe we should...."

"I think we can...."

Their words ran over each other, and his phone buzzed in his back pocket. Annoyed, he had to slip his hand free and pull the damn device out. The message splashed icy reality over his desire. "Get dressed."

He stood, grabbed her bag from where he'd dropped it, and walked to the sliding glass door, shutting it and pulling the drapes.

"What's wrong?" But she scooted forward, pulling her T-shirt down and dragging on a pair of shorts. Standing, she tugged her hair up into a ponytail and looked all of sixteen. It didn't help he knew she was in her late twenties—he suddenly felt very much like a letch.

"duMonde's on his way here."

She froze and stared at him. "Impossible."

"No, my guy is right behind him and said duMonde left his Beverly Hills hotel with three cars. duMonde is on his way to Pasadena." He cursed his own libido, searching the room and throwing all of their stuff together in one collection. He left the waiter's jacket hanging in the closet. Using a towel from the bathroom, he started wiping down all the surfaces he'd touched—including the coffee mugs.

"Okay, you wiping all traces of us away isn't disturbing at all."

He glanced over and found her staring at him with a frown. "I'll explain later."

"You know...if you didn't want to have sex, you could have said so."

He finished wiping the table and walked over to her. Sliding his fingers into the waistband of her shorts, he pulled her close and pressed her right against the stiffness of his dick trying to escape his pants. "I want to have sex. I want to have a lot of sex—hot, wet, naked sex. But, right now, the priority is keeping you out of duMonde's reach."

"He won't find me here." She seemed adamant.

"You're right. He won't because we're going to your house in Malibu."

The heat in her gaze turned to frost. "No, we're not."

"Yes, we are. You may not like it and you may not want to be there, but, since you never stay on the property, no one will think to look for you there." He took her arm and did a visual double check of the room. "Get your purse."

"Stop giving me orders." She pulled out of his grasp and glared at him. "We are not going to Malibu."

He sighed. "We can argue about this in the car. But you wanted a couple of days...."

She bit her lip and turned away, stuffing a travel pack of tissues into her purse. "I need to be in Pasadena tomorrow."

"You don't have it yet." He swore internally.

"No. I told you I don't."

"But it will be here tomorrow."

"I didn't say that either."

Jarod scowled. "Do you have to be in *this* hotel?"

She said nothing, and he glanced up at the ceiling, calming the rapid beat of his heart with a series of deep breaths.

"You need to trust me." Demand underscored his plea.

"I don't know you."

They'd arrived at an impasse.

"If you don't need to be at this hotel, then we can switch and it won't matter."

"Why switch if he's searching every hotel? We increase the chances of running into him." She wasn't wrong, except she checked herself into this one.

"The night clerk saw you, and, even in those baggy clothes and hat, you're worth remembering." He didn't think too hard about what noticing her meant or why he felt the need to say it. "Trust me for five minutes to get you out of here and somewhere safe then you can go right back to keeping me at arm's length."

She slanted a look at the bed.

"Okay, so you can keep me at panty's length." He grinned despite the tension coiling through his gut. Whether it was greed or competition driving duMonde, he'd fixated on Kit, and the last place she needed to be was in his direct line of fire.

"And this could all be a ruse to lure me out into the open where he can grab me." She folded her arms and retreated another step. "If you want me to go, you let me go. You back off, you run interference—whatever it is you want to do—but you give me the space to do the same."

He could knock her out and carry her out of here in less time than this argument took. Or he could tell her the truth.

The phone buzzed with another update. duMonde was roughly three miles away at a hotel closer to the freeway. She didn't flinch from his stare or back off on her stance. Her poker face probably netted her millions in business meetings. *No wonder her father wants her to take on more of the mantle of control.*

"What if we call a cease fire? It's not a truce, and it's not an admission of trust. We move the board from one location to another and we play again."

"You don't get it, do you? You manage to infiltrate a meeting of high level bankers and executives involved in Hardwicke Industries. You board my plane without my consent or my knowledge. You track me when I purposefully disposed of any possible electronic surveillance device and invite yourself into my hotel room and start giving me orders. I have no idea if Jarod Parker is even your name. I may be impulsive and reckless at times, but I am not stupid. So, no, Mr. Parker. I may have entertained your seduction, but I am not walking a foot outside the door without more assurance than some bogus cease-fire offer from a professional imposter." Every sentence chipped away at his ego, but he gave her credit—she nailed him on the last accusation.

"Fine." He flipped his phone to the keypad and dialed an international number by heart, not bothering to disguise the identity of the name appearing on the screen. It rang twice.

"*Bonjour, Monsieur* Curry!" Sophie's exuberant greeting dragged another smile out of him. The art history specialist never seemed put off by his Walter persona's gruff attitude or controlled manner. If anything, it made her warmer and friendlier.

"*Bonjour*, Sophie. How is Paris treating you?" He stared right at Kit as he spoke, his voice changing, adopting Walter's more formal tones. Shock rippled through the distrust on her face, and her eyes narrowed.

"I am in love with Louvre. I could live there." A masculine voice in the background grumbled, and Jarod listened to the stream of French curses.

"Is Pietr well?"

"Oh, he's fine. He's insisted on building a crib at every apartment or house we stay in. I think this one is getting the better of him, though." She laughed as Pietr cursed again. "But, yes, I'm sure it will be wonderful when the baby gets here and we *never* stop traveling from city to city." The roll of her eyes echoed in her voice.

"Sophie, I need a favor."

"Oh?" Intrigue filled Sophie's hushed tone. "Anya says you

never ask for favors."

"Anya is correct. But I need you to vouch for me to a friend of yours."

"Of course, I'd be happy to. Are you in New York?" Curiosity practically bubbled in her voice.

"No, not at the moment. Let me put Lady Katherine Hardwicke on—" He didn't get to finish before Sophie burst out laughing.

"Sorry, sorry. Yes, please put her on. And no, Pietr, I don't think I could put it together better than you. I promise." But the amusement in her voice decried the denial. Jarod held the phone out to Kit, and she had to step toward him to take it.

"Hello?" She studied him as she listened to the sudden burst of conversation from Sophie.

"I see." Her eyebrows rose, and she looked him over. "Describe him to me."

He said nothing, letting Sophie tell her he was a man in his mid-fifties, slightly balding, with salt-and-pepper hair, a thick jaw, and a gently rounding belly. His slightly hooked nose would be labeled a throwback to his Native American blood.

"Interesting. Thank you, Sophie. I do appreciate it. Oh, you do have Pietr wound up, don't you?" She could be an actress, her voice perfectly modulated to a friendly casual without any intimation of stress. Sophie continued to chatter, but Kit interrupted. "I'm so very glad you like it, and I look forward to our next luncheon. In the meanwhile, we have to go into a meeting. Yes, darling. I told you we would be fabulous friends."

A few more sentences and they rang off, but Kit held onto his phone. "You're Walter Curry?"

"Yes, ma'am."

"A fifty-year-old with a bald spot and a thickening waist." She rubbed her tongue against her teeth. "Which one is the mask, Walter or Jarod?"

"Walter."

His phone buzzed in her hand, and she passed it back without looking at the screen. "Okay. I'll go with you."

"Good, because duMonde is here." *Dammit, I should have knocked her out.*

"That's fine. We only need to move rooms." She scooped her duffel away from him and walked to the door. He barely got there in time to brace it closed and nudged her back.

"Me first." He looked out and scanned the hallway, quiet save for the muffled sound of an ice machine. "If we go down the stairs...."

But Kit didn't follow him. She walked across the hall to the other door.

"We don't have time to try and break in, and those electronic doors are harder to crack than—"

The door opened in thirty seconds, and she glanced at him. "You were saying?"

The elevator dinged its arrival, and Jarod hustled her inside, closing the door as silently as he could manage. The dark room was—thankfully—unoccupied. He leaned against the door and watched their room through the peephole.

duMonde and three of his men slotted a key in the room they'd left and burst inside. Kit moved up beside him, but he held up two fingers for silence. The men weren't long. Louis stomped out and looked both ways up and down the corridor.

"She's still here." duMonde looked down at a black device in his hand. "Go down and question the clerk again then get his master key. I want men on each entrance and exit."

"Sir, if we push too hard, someone might call the cops again."

His face a mask of fury, the Frenchman rounded on the speaker and they backed off, hands raised. "We're on it."

The group moved off, and Jarod swung a look at Kit. She wasn't wearing anything she'd had on earlier. The duffel bag she claimed at the bus station, so what the hell could duMonde be tracking?

He replayed the scene at the airport...the way duMonde seized her face and pulled her in for the kiss to each cheek.

Son of a bitch. Nudging her into the bathroom, he pressed a finger to her lips then shut the door and cut off the lights. He flicked through the applications on his phone until he found the black light. Turning it on, he waved the phone over her cheek.

His blood went cold.

Fingerprints glowed against her cheek.

The bastard tagged her with a radioactive isotope.

"Okay," she whispered. "I think I might need your help."

Chapter Seven

T hree hours later, they were back on the freeway and merging into Sunday morning traffic. It took some finesse to get out of the hotel, but Jarod settled for pulling the fire alarm and mingling with the early morning crowd in their borrowed hotel robes. They shuffled through with everyone, weaved around the fire trucks, and reclaimed Jarod's car from the lot. Hopefully, the three hundred irritated guests and hotel employees kept Louis busy while they escaped.

"Where are we heading?" She tried not to focus on the fact they left Pasadena in the rearview mirror. She couldn't go anywhere near the post box with the radiation on her face.

Her face.

"Disneyland." Of all the destinations he could have named, her man of a thousand faces picked the Happiest Place on Earth.

"Crowds. Early morning opening hours. Backstage area." He ticked off the items. "Harder to track you there, and security won't let them in with guns. So it buys us some time."

"To do what exactly?" She hadn't thought she'd really needed his help right up until he used the black light to illuminate the greenish fingerprints glowing on her skin. A shudder raced up her spine.

"To neutralize the tracing element. If it's a standard tracer, it's got an eight day half-life."

Her heart sank. "Eight days?"

His hand covered hers. It wasn't the first time he'd gone for the comforting gesture, but she really appreciated it this time. "It's going to be fine. Now we know it's there, we can get it removed."

"You're extremely casual about all of this. Run into radioactive isotopes on a regular basis, do you?" She tried for flippant, but her tone sounded harsher than she intended. Jarod stroked her wrist with his thumb, rubbing soothing circles over her pulse.

"Actually, I do. Skin contact for less than forty-eight hours won't have any lasting detrimental effects."

The steel bands caging her chest squeezed. "And longer than forty-eight?"

"As far as I know, most standard tracers are safe for the half-life they're assigned. You might get a headache or some nausea—"

"Or a severe lack of appetite?" She was not a hypochondriac or easily spooked...but radiation? It freaked her out, and she wasn't ashamed to admit it.

"You weren't hungry on the flight out from New York. Stress is more effective at killing an appetite than a tracer is."

She twisted sideways in the car to look at him. The gentle caress of his thumb helped; her pulse stopped racing like a filly fresh out of the gate at the Derby. "And how the hell are you a fifty-year-old man who Sophie knows?"

"I told you. I am familiar with hiding in plain sight."

She waited, and, when he said nothing else, she reached over and pinched him.

He gave her an amused look. "Yes?"

"You didn't answer my question."

"No, but you've had enough truth from me for today. I gave you a secret. It's customary for you to give me one." How he could be so relaxed as they cruised through ever thickening traffic she couldn't fathom. His gaze occasionally flicked to the rearview mirror, but she didn't imagine he saw much because he wasn't reacting.

"Does Sophie know you're...well, you're you under the Walter Curry?"

He shook his head once.

"Does anyone know?" She fished for more information. The act betrayed her curiosity, but, damn it, he intrigued her.

"One other and now you."

"That's it?" Okay, a larger secret than she'd expected. She blew out a breath and looked down at their joined hands.

"Yes. I am hoping you will choose to keep the information to yourself, but I won't ask you to."

"I have no reason to expose you." She wouldn't promise not to.

She lived in the real world where leverage could reduce fallout. She glanced behind them, studying the various cars. Why so many were thronging into Anaheim so early, she didn't see the point. She'd never been a fan of amusement parks.

"No sign of a tail yet. But he may not need one."

"Because he can track my face." She gritted her teeth. Invasive bastard, he'd grabbed her face at the airport for more than a threat— he'd done it so he could follow her. *Did he plan to beat the location out of me and, barring that, let me go with the hope I'd run after it?*

"Kit?"

"No, Jarod. I am not answering the question."

"duMonde's had people killed to get his hands on the Buddha. He had Sophie attacked, twice, and kidnapped. His men shot Pietr."

She didn't flinch at the revelation. She'd been there. She'd seen them in the aftermath, Pietr worn to a frayed end and Sophie still and pale in the hospital. That they'd managed to work it out bolstered her faith in the human species, but it didn't change the fact she couldn't answer.

It wasn't only her secret.

"Who are you protecting?"

"Myself. My company. My family's reputation."

He followed a stream of other cars steadily into an oversized lot. They parked in the Pluto lot, and he glanced at her duffel. "Anything you need from the bag?"

"Other than a wardrobe change and some makeup? No, I'm fine." She refused to look at her appearance in the mirror. Instead, she pulled out the ponytail holder, finger combed her hair back, and fixed it up again. Based on the various outfits on the crowds beginning their walks to the tram, her shorts and T-shirt blended right in. Jarod and his casual business wear on the other hand.... Before she could say anything, he pulled a solar shield from behind her seat and spread it out across the window. Most of those who'd parked when they did were already gone, rushing off to their happy place.

Jarod unbuttoned his shirt and stripped down to a dark tank top underneath. He sported one large tattoo on his left shoulder, some Native American symbols and squares. The muscles in his arms rippled with every gesture. He toed off his shoes and reached behind him for a pair of flip-flops, and, when his hands went to his belt, she unbuckled her seat belt to watch.

Despite his large size, he slid out of the dress pants. A pair of black boxers hugged his thighs and did nothing to disguise the semi-erection he sported. He twisted in the seat and dumped the pants and button down in a bag and pushed them under the passenger seat. Next, he pulled out a smaller bag and a pair of khaki shorts. He slid those on, and she bit her lip when he thrust his hips up to pull them over his ass.

He buttoned them up, pulled the tank top out to hang over the top of the waistband, and slid his sunglasses back into place.

"Holy crap."

"Thank you." He slid out of the driver's side. She fumbled with the door handle and scooped up her purse to follow him. The aviator glasses, with their steel rims, the tattoo, and the ripped muscles on display in his arms and legs gave him the look of a very dangerous surfer.

But he didn't even look like the man who drove the car.

"How do you do it?" She circled the car and took the hand he held out to her. The car alarm beeped as he activated it, and they set off across the blazing parking lot, already warming under the California sunshine.

"Attitude. Over half of all perception is based on how a person walks, talks, and delivers their body language cues. It's also partly the clothes and the style of dress." He nudged her between two cars, and they walked over to the other lane to avoid oncoming traffic. "People see a tattoo and they make a snap judgment. The rest of their impressions will follow their first snapshot. The same can be said for a suit...or a pair of thousand dollar Jimmy Choos."

She understood the theory. Dressing for success was not only a mantra, but a truism. Whether a potential employee seeking a job or a woman on a first date, how she dressed and carried herself made an impression. The impression offered the foundation for all other expectations.

"And you learned how to do this to recover stolen art?"

"No, I learned how to do this to assassinate people and gather intelligence." The calm, almost casual way he said the words sent a cold chill down her spine and a spark of electricity from her nipples to her sex.

"Okay, knowing that shouldn't be sexy." She meant the words more for herself than for him, but he gave her a wink then nodded to the crowd. Time to table the conversation for a more private venue.

Children danced in place and chattered while smiling parents and grandparents indulged them. They likely wouldn't be in another ten hours, but, for now, the cluster of humanity surged with anticipation.

His face relaxed from the shrewd, assessing mask he normally wore. Instead, a relaxed smile came readily to his lips, and he glanced at her frequently. When the tram arrived, he guided her onto a bench in the center, while he took the outside position. A college-aged boy slid in next to her and bumped her leg. Jarod wrapped an arm around her shoulders and looked at the kid until he scooted over, leaving a five-inch divide between him and Kit.

She didn't laugh, but it took some effort. An interesting ferry ride. The kids grew even more excited as the tram motored through the parking lot, and then they were at the park gates and the mad dash inside began in earnest.

It might be early on a Sunday, but the crowds swarmed.

"There must be hundreds of people here."

"Try thousands. Nothing safer than a crowd."

Rather than remove his arm from her shoulders, he kept her close, particularly as the throngs tightened at the check in. He followed her through the purse search line and to the turnstiles. Inside, he slid his hand down her arm until their fingers interlaced, and they strolled through the shops lining Main Street.

He bought new shirts—a Donald for him and a Daisy for her. She rolled her eyes but changed obediently. When he held up the mouse ears, she balked, and he kissed her nose. Her heart flip-flopped at the casual intimacy of the gesture. They picked up sodas and French fries and fed most of them to the birds while the first parade of the day played through.

Their path took a circuitous route. They paused for pictures in a couple of places, and he accepted the photo pass card from the photographer. She couldn't figure out where they were going or what he searched for. They watched a show in front of the castle, rode the carousel, paused for photographs with oversized chipmunks, and waded through a thick crowd heading into the self-proclaimed adventure area.

When he pointed to the log ride, she stared at him.

"Do you have any idea what the water is going to do to my hair?" It may not be styled or looking particularly elegant, but with her curls, any kind of moisture could turn her hair upside down. *No, thank you.*

"Trust me." He led her up the ramp, and they stood in line for nearly fifteen minutes as it inched forward. At a break in the line, a man waved them to the express route even though they didn't have tickets. Jarod held her hand as they passed the others in the standard line, and, when it curved away from them, he pressed a hand to the wall and a section of it swung inward like a door.

She had no time to gape before they walked inside and down a short flight of stairs to a small room with several computers and a middle-aged man dressed in Bermuda shorts, a red Hawaiian shirt, and pair of loafers.

"Jarod. Good to see you." The two men shook hands. "And this is?"

"You don't need her name," Jarod replied drily.

"Do I need his?" Kit asked, because, as surreal went, they'd arrived.

"No. You don't." He led her to a chair and pulled it out. "It's on her right cheek."

"Got it." The man pulled out a black light and flicked off the overhead with a remote. He held it up to her face and studied her silently. "I need to get a sample. It's a small scraping and it won't hurt."

The lights came back on, but Jarod took the small instrument and brushed her cheek with it. He handed the slide to the tech, and the man carried it to his computer. He hummed along with the music she could hear faintly in the background.

"Okay." He pulled a pair of reading glasses off his head and peered at the screen. "I have some good news, and I have some bad news."

"Bad news." She and Jarod spoke at the same time.

The tech turned around with a wry look. "The crap to get the isotope off stinks. But it's pretty effective, and we can reduce the trace signature in no time."

"Okay, so what's the good news?" Jarod stared at him.

"Well, the good news is whoever is using this probably got it from a Scandium 45 derivative from an old Stasi project mothballed in the mid-1980s. A cache of it was stolen from a research facility in Austria a couple of weeks ago. It's been red flagged." The man shrugged.

"How does that help me?" No disguising her frown at the

information.

"Well, when a shark is hunting you, good to know there's another shark on its tail." Another shrug, but he sounded pleased with himself.

"Will it scar?" She didn't really care about the Stasi or Louis' ever-evolving resume of criminal acts.

"No. Just stink. You need to get a compound of.... You know, you probably don't want to know." He wrote something down on a sheet of paper. "Give me a minute and I'll see if I can track some down. Most of the park includes heavy metal pieces, so it's going to provide you with a lot of shielding. They might know you came inside, but they won't be able to track you unless they're standing on top of you."

"Thanks," Jarod said, and the man nodded, heading to his secret door and stepping out.

Kit glanced up at him. "The U.S. government is operating a secret listening post inside an amusement park? Doesn't it violate a half-dozen privacy laws?"

"This isn't a listening post."

"But he's an agent, right?"

"Never said he was." Jarod walked to a small refrigerator and opened it. He pulled out two bottles of water and handed her one.

"So what is this place?"

Jarod glanced around and shrugged. "Tech support for the ride." He unscrewed the bottle and took a drink. "I told you I could help."

"I know."

"But you still don't trust me." It wasn't a question, and she couldn't give him false assurances. She wanted to trust him—which was more than she could say for when he showed up in her hotel room or tried to talk her into leaving with him.

But she'd been doing this on her own for far too long.

"I'm sorry." She meant it, too.

"Trust takes time," he agreed.

It did, and she didn't understand why he'd shared a secret with her, unless he was ready to leave his alias behind. She wanted to ask him about his comment before they arrived at the tram—about training to gather information and assassinate people. But, at the same time, she didn't want to know.

"Kit?"

She looked at him.

"You doing okay over there?"

"I'm fine." No, she wasn't, but it sounded better than "I'm ready to freak the hell out now. Do you mind waiting while I run around in circles and scream?"

Her face itched, but she tried to ignore it and opened her bottle to drink. The hum of the machines grated on her nerves, but she distanced herself from the sound. On the run in the middle of an amusement park with radiation eating away at her face or sitting at a party for five hundred businessmen and celebutantes, the etiquette prevailed—maintain her calm.

The door burst open, and their red-shirted technician returned with a small jar. "And here is the stinky crap. It's got a small amount of lead in it, so you might get some redness on your face, but it will neutralize the compound, and you'll be isotope free lickety-split." He finished his statement with a flourish and unscrewed the cap.

The smell hit her like a hammer—a combination of something soggy and decaying mixed with heavy metals and cold cream. Her stomach lurched, and Jarod jerked the pot away from her face. "Harry."

"Sorry, man." He looked sheepish, but she concentrated on breathing through her mouth rather than taking another whiff of the gunk they wanted her to put on her face. Using toxic waste to remove radiation. She led a charmed life.

Taking the jar from Jarod's hand, she looked to Harry. "How long does it have to stay on my face?"

"Five, no more than ten minutes. Then wash it off thoroughly. There's a restroom right there." He pointed to a door partly hidden behind one of his half-walls of computers.

She nodded. "Thank you."

"Hey, let me help." Jarod touched her arm, but she shook her head at him.

"Someone should be conscious if I pass out from the fumes." Shut inside the tiny bathroom, she turned on the water. She glanced at herself in the mirror. The woman looking back at her really seemed nothing at all like the lady who'd graced the cover of a recent *Sun-Times* article. She opened the jar before she could change her mind and used a folded up tissue to apply it to her cheek.

Cold, clammy, and disgusting.

She glanced at her watch and screwed the lid back on the jar.

Outside the bathroom, the men murmured in voices too low for her to quite make out. Probably catching up. She fished one of the burner phones out of her purse. She had two left. The other two were still in the car they were most likely abandoning.

Dialing Enrique's number, she left the water running.

He answered on the second ring. "I am not going to ask why you are at Disneyland."

"Good. I don't really want to discuss it."

He laughed. "You are calling for the profile, yes?"

"Yes please."

"Jarod Parker does not exist. Well, let me rephrase this, he does exist, but he is so blandly ordinary he cannot be a real person."

"What do you mean?" Her eyes watered, and she looked at her watch. Six minutes to go.

"Exactly what I said. He's been scrubbed, from top to bottom. No details about family, average high school career, even more average college, a brief stint in law school—where he didn't graduate—and, after, a desk job in a Midwest banking establishment. He's...ordinary."

No, he's extraordinary. "Is it a cover?"

"*Si, senorita.* Are you in trouble?"

She coughed and squinted her eyes shut against the burn. "I am fine, Enrique. Thank you for looking into this."

"Katerina"—he was the only person on Earth who called her that—"I can be in Los Angeles by tomorrow morning."

"No." She sniffed as her nose began to run along with her eyes. She peered at her watch. Two minutes left. "But I may need to vacation in a few days.... How is the weather there?"

"Balmy skies, warm sunshine, and all the seclusion a body could desire. Call me when you are ready."

Message sent. Message received.

She had a place to run to if she needed it.

"*Gracias, Enrique.*"

"*De nada, señorita.*"

They rang off, and she swayed before stripping out the sim card and dropping it into the toilet and flushing it. The rest of the phone went into the trash. Jarod knocked on the door.

"Kit?"

"Washing it off now. I can barely breathe, so I recommend getting away from the door when I open it."

She scrubbed at her face with the water, peeling away the goopy gel-like substance the cream had become. It plopped into the sink, and she gagged. She barely made it to the toilet before she brought up the few French fries she'd managed to eat earlier.

A strong arm braced her and held her up. When the retching passed, Jarod flushed the toilet and grabbed the washcloth. He sat her on the closed toilet lid and went to cleaning her face. She could barely see him around the tears rolling down her cheeks.

Harry appeared with a fan and set it up blowing cold air into the stench of the bathroom. She couldn't breathe through her nose at all now, so she had no idea if it was helping. Three more scrubs with soap and water and Jarod led her out. She dabbed at her eyes repeatedly, but they were swollen and sore.

"Yeah, it stinks. That's the only problem with it!" Jarod's voice was cold and hostile.

She squinted to see which of them he spoke to, but he stared at Harry.

"Like I said...it's got a bad smell. She probably shouldn't have shut the bathroom door. It contained all of it in a small place. But it's only a little toxic—"

She couldn't help it, she laughed. The sound came out like a strangled sob, and she dabbed her eyes again. "A little toxic. Is it like being a little pregnant?"

"Well, yes and no. You feel like crap, but it won't kill you." Harry retreated when Jarod took a step toward him. "I'm serious. She'll be fine. The worst is she looks like a massive case of hay fever. Grab some antihistamines, and it will clear up. But check her face with the black light, isotope is all gone."

"You know, I don't even care anymore." She really couldn't breathe. *Ridiculous.* She blew her nose and accepted a fresh tissue from Jarod. The lights turned off, and she waited while they put the black light on her.

"It's gone," Jarod confirmed.

"Well, at least it was worth it. Now you can be rid of me." The flip remark came out a lot whinier and more pathetic than intended. She sighed and took a long drink from the water bottle Jarod pressed into her hands.

"We'll talk when we're out of here." He looked back at Harry. "Did you get us a car?"

"Yep, Mickey lot, slot five. I'll take care of yours and get it cleaned and dropped back at the airport. Want me to dead drop any gear in it?"

They both shook their heads. "No."

She wheezed a laugh, but at least the watery eyes slowly abated. She didn't want to even begin looking at herself. They left Harry a few minutes later and went back to the line then down an exit staircase for employees. Their circuitous route through the park took a more direct line to the gates and then out again. They didn't pause to sight see.

In the Mickey lot, they found a four door tan SUV. Twenty minutes later, they were back on a freeway and so ready to go to sleep, but they didn't have time for rest.

"Pasadena?"

She said nothing. Her insides twisted, her face hurt, her eyes burned, and her soul ached. The only bright spot in the last twenty-four hours sat right next to her, but she couldn't trust it.

She couldn't trust him.

"Yes, please." She licked her lips and reached for the water bottle again. "If I ask you a question, will you tell me the truth?"

"As much as I am able." It wasn't an unfair answer.

"Why do you want the Buddha?"

"Because I want to return it to where it belongs—the temple in Thailand. It is a treasured piece of their cultural and artistic history. It should go home."

"And that's it?" She pulled her knee up to her chest and stared out the window, not at him. She wanted to hear the honesty in his voice—the man could play too many expressions, be too many people. He was some kind of government spy or had been at one time.

"That's it."

"So if I promise to help you facilitate your desire, can you give me twenty-four hours?"

"Kit...."

"Seriously, Jarod. You name the place, and I will be there in twenty-four hours. But I need some time...and then I'll...I'll help you return the Buddha to where it belongs."

They drove another five miles before he spoke. "Who are you protecting, Kit?"

"If I tell you, then I'm not protecting them anymore."

"Then tell me what you can—"

She cut a look at him.

"I told you I would help you take your two days, and I meant it. duMonde is still out there, and when he figures out we thwarted his little tracer, he's going to get meaner. So leaving you to fend for yourself.... It's not going to happen. I can look the other way and not see anything if you need discretion, but I need you to tell me what you can so I know what you need."

"I want to trust you." She really did.

"Then, read me in. Tell me what you can, and I promise you, I will help you make happen whatever it is you need to make happen."

He didn't touch her, but he didn't have to. His presence in the car wrapped around her like a blanket, and damn if she didn't want to snuggle into it. She'd known him less than forty-eight hours. How was it possible she wanted to trust him?

"At sixteen years old, I found out my mother was alive." It sounded rather ridiculous in some ways. She wasn't sure where else to start this story, though.

"And this was news to you?"

"Yes. Until then, I thought she died when I was born. But it turned out to be a lie my father told me to protect me." She hesitated again. Only two people in the world knew the truth about what happened in those two weeks after her sixteenth birthday. Her father because he had to help her pick up the pieces.

"Why did he have to protect you?"

"Because she was—is—a drug addict. Cocaine, alcohol, and pills. An aspiring actress when my father met her, they had a whirlwind affair. He knew she indulged recreationally, but he didn't realize the extent of the problem until she was pregnant. After she gave birth, she used to forget about me because she would be drinking or popping her pills. When I was a few months old, she apparently left to go on a bender and didn't tell anyone I needed a babysitter. Daddy found me about twelve hours later, screaming my head off in an empty house because she'd given the staff the night off."

She distanced herself from this part of the story. Her father's nightmare—his face went gray when he told her about it, anger and revulsion evident. "He divorced her almost immediately and had her parental rights terminated. Well, actually, he told her she could go into rehab or she could get out. She chose to stick to her drugs. He didn't tell me the last part, though."

The silence stretched between them.

"Who told you then, Kit?"

"She did." She blew out a breath. "And my grandfather—her father—confirmed it." Her grandfather, the only other man who knew her secret, the retired jewel thief with a dying wish she would grant if it killed her.

And at the rate they were going, it might.

Chapter Eight

V ery little emotional inflection echoed beneath the words as she spoke about her mother. Her relationship, tenuous at best, didn't survive their first meeting. At sixteen, the pampered daughter of a wealthy diplomat and industrialist probably didn't have the reserves to combat such profound disappointment. In the years since, she'd armored herself against the memory.

It was what survivors did.

He didn't probe for more information about her mother. The memory, a defining moment for her to be sure, also proved a distraction. A truth hidden behind another truth, and he couldn't fault her. He trusted few. That every instinct and shred of research he turned up on Lady Hardwicke added fuel to the trust his gut already held for the woman aside, she was right—he'd revealed his hand to get her to reveal hers.

By the time he pulled off at the first Pasadena exit and found a quiet side street to park on, she stared out the window. Slipping the car into park, he tapped her leg lightly. "Let's see how your face is."

She turned, and he could almost feel the weight of her gaze despite the sunglasses shrouding her eyes. Her right cheek looked burned, the skin bright pink, a circular stamp from where she'd rubbed the cream.

He didn't like it, but the skin didn't show any signs of rupture or break. Reddened and uncomfortable, he was sure, but not long-term threatening. He stroked the skin below it. "Hurt?"

"No. It's sore and a little raw. But I've had worse sunburns while on holiday in the Mediterranean." The small smile didn't quite touch both corners of her mouth, but he let the little lie go.

"Eyes?"

She lifted the sunglasses. Her eyes were bloodshot, red rimmed, and swollen. He grimaced. "We should probably get you some cold cloths."

"In a little while." She put the glasses back on and glanced at her watch.

The tick-tock sensation returned. Jarod drummed his hands against the steering wheel. "Two hours."

"I need twelve."

"Three."

Her lips pursed. "Nine."

"Five." He looked at her. "And we're pushing it."

"If you're going to trust me with five, why not twelve?" Her hands clenched into white-knuckled fists.

"If you want me to trust you, why don't you show a little trust of your own? duMonde is still out there. He doesn't need one hour or twelve, he needs one second. One second you're alone and unprotected to grab you, to shoot you...." He leaned back in the seat. He couldn't force her to trust him. He couldn't hold her captive, either, no matter how much he wanted to tuck her away somewhere safe while he dealt with duMonde.

Seventy-two hours to go from hunter to hunted. Seventy-two hours to turn a professional challenge into a personal vendetta. He'd left the field for a reason, and this current emotional investment clouded his judgment. Maybe he needed to back off, assign another agent. He dismissed the idea before it could fully form.

"Five twelve Brewer."

"What?" The odd response dragged him away from the internal turmoil.

"We're five and five now, so five twelve Brewer." She didn't look at him with the last, exhaling it on a hard breath as though saying it out loud proved far more difficult than she'd anticipated.

He stared at her. "We're six and four. How are you figuring five and five?"

She pursed her lips. "You told me about Walter Curry. Point to me."

"I found the radioactive isotope and got rid of it for you. Point to me."

"I got us into the locked room and pulled the fire alarm to get out of the building. Point to me."

A reluctant grin tugged at the corner of his mouth. He still wanted to know how she'd bypassed the electronic lock so quickly. "I got rid of the tracer and got us a new car. Point to me."

She rubbed her chin. "Okay, seven and six."

"Seven and six." The tension in his shoulders eased. "Five twelve Brewer?"

"Yep."

He reversed out of their parking spot and programmed the address into his GPS. "What's at five twelve Brewer?"

"A place." Amusement punctuated the answer.

"So, now we're reduced to twenty questions. Should I ask if we're there yet?" Another knot in his spine unlocked, and he leaned back in his seat and claimed her hand. She glanced at their interlocked fingers, and, when he tugged her hand over to rest against his leg, she squeezed once.

"Actually, you're driving, so I should be the one asking if we're there yet."

"True." He conceded the point. "So is it a public place?"

She laughed. "Yes."

The address was seven blocks from where he pulled off the freeway and sat squarely in the middle of a tired strip mall. The wrinkles of time and a losing battle with the elements pitted the blacktop with potholes and crisscrossed the sidewalks with cracks. He parked right in front of the storefront boasting the number on its front door. A metal gate barricaded the inside of the glass, and no signs labeled the storefront sandwiched between a pizza joint advertising five dollar pies and a salon boasting ten dollar haircuts.

Putting the car in park, he paused.

"Come on." She opened the car door then slid out.

He shut off the car and followed suit. Outside the vehicle, he scanned the empty parking lot, closed storefronts, and the intermittent passing traffic. Kit stood on the sidewalk, waiting.

He followed her to the entrance, while she tapped in a code. The lock hummed open, and the interior gate unlocked and parted wide enough to allow one person through at a time. Refraining from comment, he pulled the door open and waved her through. Inside, she walked to another keypad and punched in a second set of numbers. It locked, and the gate slid back together—sealing them in.

The oblong room included two copy machines, paper products,

and a customer counter. Kit walked back to a number of private gold-faced boxes lining the far wall. Three cameras monitored the room, but none showed red or green lights indicating operation. Jarod followed her, splitting his attention between her destination and the entrance. A storefront like this likely had rear access, but it seemed to be hidden behind the customer counter and the shelves decorating the back wall.

At the series of boxes, she pressed her thumb to a fingerprint scanner and a small keypad slid out. She hit a combination of numbers and four boxes swung out, revealing they were a faux front for a safe door.

"Nice." He admired clever craftsmanship. "Do you own this place?"

"A subdivision of a shell of a shell." She slid out a thick envelope and a plain cardboard box.

"You mailed it...." Astonishment turned to pride. "Brilliant."

"Thank you." She shifted the weight of the box and stacked the envelope on top of it. Sealing the door shut, she led him around behind the customer counter to a small office tucked against the wall, out of sight of the main doors.

Addressed to the receiving shop, the box bore a return address of New York and an NYPD stamp on the postage paid. Pride at the absolute simplification of removing the Buddha from lockup grew in his chest. She hadn't needed to sneak it out of the building—the post office did it for her.

She slit open the manila envelope first. Out came a wallet, a stack of cash, and a cell phone. She slid the cell phone into her purse, without turning it on, along with the cash and then flipped open the wallet. He counted four credit cards and a driver's license, all in her name.

Satisfied, she snapped it shut and added it to her purse before zipping the whole thing shut. She dropped the envelope in a shredder then placed her hand on the box. "Okay, now what?"

"You still have another thirty hours or so." His palms itched to open the box and confirm its contents, but he'd given her his word, and she'd let him come this far.

"If we take this out of here, you can be charged as an accessory after the fact." The closest she'd come to a confession in this game.

"You let me worry about it. Where do you need to go now?" Trust required a leap of faith, one he'd already made.

"Bakersfield."

He did some mental calculations. "Two hours from here. When do we need to be there?"

"I need to make a phone call before I can give you an answer. But I need privacy to make the call."

He studied her; she didn't look away and she didn't flinch.

"Okay. If you'll let me out, I'll wait in the car." He didn't miss her blink of surprise or the ripple of relief easing the tension her expression. He ignored the box and turned to walk to the door. She followed him and pressed the code on the keypad. He didn't look back at her until he slid behind the wheel of the car. The gates closed, and she disappeared behind the customer service desk.

She could run. Just because he hadn't seen the rear entrance didn't mean there wasn't one. She could go out the back door, carrying her prize, slip into a car she'd stashed, and disappear. He slid the keys into the ignition but didn't turn the car on.

The hardest part of a mission was not deciding when to act but when not to. At this stage of their game, she trusted him or she didn't. Ten minutes later, she rewarded his patience by exiting the building, box in hand. She locked up, opened the back door of the SUV, and tucked the box behind her seat. He waited until she climbed into the passenger side and glanced back at the box.

The seal didn't appear broken. It had the same address and stamp mark. But she could have replaced it, removed the Buddha and—

He cut the direction of those thoughts off. Trust meant believing she didn't seek to deceive him.

"Thank you," she murmured in an almost melancholy voice.

"You're welcome." He continued to practice patience, backing out of the parking spot and heading for the highway before asking, "When do we need to be in Bakersfield?"

"What?" She glanced at him. She'd left her sunglasses perched on her head, and the sadness in her green eyes tore at his heart.

"When do we need to be there, Kit Kat?"

"Tomorrow morning." She swallowed and looked away from him again. It was midafternoon, and they still had a two-hour drive in front of them. "I didn't realize how late in the day it had gotten."

"We'll get a hotel, some fresh clothes, and dinner—maybe not in that order. What time tomorrow morning?"

"Eight sharp."

He looked at his watch. It gave them about sixteen hours. He accelerated onto the on ramp and kept his attention divided between her and their route. She folded her arms and leaned her head against the glass. The quiet loneliness dragged at his soul and worried him. Fifteen minutes later, he reached over to pull her limp hand into his. Flattening her palm against his bare leg, he stroked a path around her knuckles.

"Will you tell me why you pretend to be someone else for Pietr and Sophie?"

He barely heard her quiet question. "I don't pretend to be someone else for them, specifically. It's how they know me."

"But why?" Real curiosity populated her question.

Answering her honestly was his only option. "Because some things are easier done when no one knows who you really are."

"Yeah, I get it." She roused from her pensive stupor. "I've had to do it more than once myself."

"I would think you do it all the time—because you're not some featherheaded dilettante or a cutthroat businesswoman—but you straddle the line brilliantly when dealing with your father's business associates." Another facet he admired about her, the ease with which she maintained control over a situation without ever appearing to exert her influence.

"True. But I grew up under a microscope of security, society, and scandal. Learning to cater to expectations creates a barrier."

"Who is real and who is only a part of the cover?" He related to her dilemma. His assets wouldn't recognize Jarod on the street—not as himself. He cultivated those relationships, though, burying his real identity beneath layer after layer of distraction and redirection.

She fell silent once more, but her fingers curled against his thigh. When he glanced at her again, her eyes were closed and her head tilted back. She'd fallen asleep. He held her hand and let her rest. His phone buzzed twice during the drive, but he ignored it. He didn't want to disturb her by moving. He spotted a nice hotel off the freeway and followed the exit signs. They would swap cars before leaving, but he could take care of the trade after dark.

Parking, he let go of her hand reluctantly and checked the text messages. duMonde was in a rage and had returned to his hotel in Beverly Hills. Jarod's heart bled for him. The second text came from the asset in Malibu. He'd tracked down the identity of her mother and her maternal grandfather. The mother resided in a rehab facility in Sonoma. A shell corporation of Hardwicke Industries paid her bills.

He glanced over at Kit's slumbering face. Despite her mother's rejection, she still took care of the woman. The second screen told him exactly why they came to Bakersfield. Her grandfather resided in a long-term-care facility and suffered from congestive heart failure. He wasn't expected to live much longer. But the name gave Jarod his second real jolt on the mission.

Sebastian Kant.

Kant had served two terms for petty larceny in his youth, but not an hour more despite a very lucrative career as a jewel thief in the sixties. The man virtually fell off the map after his last job went horribly awry. Jarod thumbed the phone off. He didn't want to read any of the details. Not when the last job Kant took had involved *The Fortunate Buddha*.

"Kit Kat." He brushed a hand over her hair and down her cheek. She stirred and blinked at him. Dusk gathered outside the car, the sun hovering low over the western horizon. "We're at a hotel. I'm going to get us a couple of rooms."

"You don't need to get two," she murmured, rubbing her face and straightening.

"You sure?" His chest tightened at the implied invitation.

"Yeah. I'm sure."

"Okay. You want to come in or wait here?"

"I'll wait here. I don't think I'm really fit for public consumption." Her yawn split the sentence into a garbled mess, but he understood it. Keys in hand, he went inside, checked in, and returned in ten minutes. Cash moved a desk clerk quickly. Fifteen minutes later, he led her into their room and carried the box over to slide into the closet.

"You're really not going to open it and look, are you?" She stood in the doorway to the bathroom.

"No." He shook his head. "Not for another...twenty-two hours."

"I've never met anyone like you." She pulled her sunglasses off and tossed them onto the bathroom counter.

He needed to move away, order some food, and put her in the shower—at the very least create some distance between them. "Is that a good thing?" He narrowed the gap separating them. The red splotch on her cheek remained a violent reminder of the lengths others were willing to go to take control or use her.

"Yeah." She nodded slowly. "A really good thing."

He hooked a finger into the waistband of her shorts and tugged her away from the wall. "I've never known anyone like you either."

"I don't know if I should ask if it's a good thing." She gave him a hesitant smile, smoothing her hands over his chest. He ached to strip the fabric out of the way. He wanted her to touch him.

"It's...it's an amazing thing." The confession should have cost him, but it didn't. He'd avoided personal entanglements for years because he never knew when a call would come in or what third world country he would wake up in the next day. After he left to make a life for himself in the IAAR, he hadn't made a life for himself—he'd made one for Walter Curry, divorcing Jarod from personal commitments.

One foot out the door and always ready to go. He could walk away, disappear, and his employers and assets would have no idea where he went.

His foot wasn't out the door with Kit. The last place he wanted to go was away, to disappear and never see her again. "We're playing this for real, now, Kit Kat. Not a game, not a test for score, not a challenge to be overcome."

"I know." The two words quivered in the air between them. "After tomorrow, I'll tell you anything you want to know."

"I only need to know one thing." He didn't care if the box held a priceless artifact. He didn't care why she stole it. He didn't care what she did last week or last month. He studied her gaze, the unflinching, brilliant pair of green eyes saw everything and gave so very little away—until a person could see beyond the surface to the startlingly brilliant woman beneath. The depths of a woman he wanted to spend decades exploring.

"What do you need to know?"

"Yes or no?" He didn't miss the slight catch to her breath or the way her cheeks turned a deeper shade of pink or the way the pupils in her eyes dilated.

"That's it? That's all you want to know?"

Jarod nodded once. "That's it."

Her teeth scraped over her lower lip. "One answer."

"Only answer," he confirmed.

Fisting his shirt into her hands, she tugged him the last inch closer, mouth bare millimeters from his. "Yes."

He closed the distance. One gentle brush turned into a fusion reaction, rocketing explosive need through his body. *She said yes.* She was all he needed.

Chapter Nine

She wanted him out of his clothes, but, instead, she stood under the shower jets and scrubbed her hair. He'd kissed her until she was breathless and given her the tiniest of pushes into the bathroom. "Shower," he'd murmured. "I'll order the food."

"I'm not hungry." She refused to be ordered around and traced the line of rippling muscle beneath his shirt. He captured her hands and pulled himself free, the lust on his face dark and full of tantalizing promise.

"I didn't say the food was for you." He'd closed the door on her outraged "oh" and left her to stew for ten seconds until his low laughter softened the rejection. A rejection she didn't quite appreciate until she caught a glimpse of herself in the mirror.

She looked terrible.

A minute later, she'd thrust herself into the shower and didn't care the water hadn't quite warmed up. She soaped her hair three times then conditioned it. Her stylist would kill her when—if—she got back to him. The water had come to slow boil by the time she scrubbed soap over her breasts and down her arm. The curtain pulled back, and Jarod stood leaning against the cool tile, gloriously naked.

"Did you order dinner?" She pivoted on one foot, facing the spray and letting it splash over her breasts and sluice away the soap.

"I did. I hope you like steak." A brush of air against her back was the only warning he'd slipped into the shower behind her. Awareness skittered through her as his chest glided against her back and his erection bumped her butt. He trailed fingers down her arm to claim the loofah she'd been using, all the while guiding her to turn until he slid under the spray.

The water danced over his skin—all lean hard-corded muscle. The brief glimpses she'd seen earlier didn't do him justice. The black tattoo engulfed his left shoulder, painted like a warrior. His abdominals were a fixed, hard six-pack—chiseled as though carved from teak. He ducked his face under the water, and she leaned back against the wall. His cock jutted up toward his belly, thick and aroused. His thighs rippled with each little step, and the muscles in his calves flexed as he stretched past her to claim the shampoo.

"You were shot." She ran her fingers across his abdomen to the scar puckering his right side, a scant inch or so above his hip.

"More than once." He nodded, twisting away to show her his back. She explored the tightly packed muscle stretching across his shoulders. She found four more scars, one so close to where his heart beat beneath his ribs her own slammed in painful sympathy.

Every question coming to mind, she banished without asking, choosing to lean forward and press her lips to each puckered reminder of the wounds he'd endured. Slipping an arm around his waist, she hugged him. She wanted to feel his heart beating, and the steady cadence of its rhythm soothed her.

"How long?" The only question she allowed a voice to.

"About seven years in the field, two behind a desk." He sidled under the spray, and she went with him, enjoying the slippery way the water slid around the parts of their bodies touching. He twisted again, pulled her against his chest, and tucked his finger beneath her chin, nudging her gaze to his. "I left on good terms but had tired of the long game. I wanted—I needed something else."

"And you found it with Walter?" She didn't know him, but she understood the loneliness of an existence built upon fabrication. The house of cards may deceive others, but they could also fool the person building it until the fiction became fact.

"No." He cupped her face in his hands, the strength gentle and caring. His mouth slanted over hers, a slow, possessive kiss sending electricity zinging through her system. She forgot about the shower, the questions, and the journey to understand and reveled in the way she fit against him, his muscular body so hard to her leaner, softer frame.

When he lifted his head, she stared at him—almost dazed. He kissed her cheek then her eyelids and, finally, the tip of her nose. "Walter provided a means to an end. He is useful and resourceful and has cultivated a number of contacts, but he wasn't what I needed."

A knock at the door, and someone calling room service interrupted. Jarod stepped out and held her hand until she stood on the floor mat next to him. Slinging a towel around his hips, he opened the bathroom door. "Stay in here for a moment."

He shut her in and the moment elongated as though he'd needed to pause before opening outer door. She toweled herself off. Her nipples were almost achingly sensitive, and her body hummed from the contact with his. She wasn't interested in food, but she did take the time to run a comb through her hair, blow dry, and brush her teeth. She still looked too pale, and the red splotch too angry when she finished, but a little bit of the hotel lotion helped her feel prettier.

Opening the door, she found Jarod waiting for her, the towel wrapped around his hips and his arms folded over his chest. She peeked at him around the edge of the door. "I don't have anything to wear."

"Ahh." He tugged his towel loose and handed it to her. He seemed even more magnificent in the sterile hotel room with its cheap art deco knockoffs and cream-colored furniture. Raw. Real. Masculine. The words didn't do him justice.

She took the towel from him and pulled the door wide, not bothering for any false sense of modesty. He'd seen her in the shower. Hell, he'd already caressed her breasts. Her nipples tightened almost painfully at the memory, and she took a moment to fold the towel and set it on the counter behind her.

The room temp cool, almost too cool, against her overheated flesh. She walked out and stared at the table he'd ordered up with their dinner set with the silver toppers still in place over the meals, a bottle of wine, four bottles of water, two empty glasses, and a single white rose.

So sweet.

Desire mixed with a wave of tenderness, the potent and heady combination far more devastating than the need to wrap around him and explore what brought them both pleasure. She wasn't supposed to get attached. She'd had her share of one-night stands and brief, albeit fun, affairs through the years. Dalliances with men who wanted something from her—or her father. Using them as they used her, she always walked away with her heart unbattered and unbruised.

Glancing over her shoulder, she saw the warmth in his stern face, the unfettered confidence in those deep-brown eyes. Understanding and something more—trust—resonated through his expression. He stared at her steadily, almost gently, and when he pulled the chair out for her to sit, her insides went liquid with need.

Again, she wasn't supposed to get attached. She never did. He circled the table and sat in the chair opposite her, his legs stretching out to tangle with hers. It amped up the need and the sense of power flowing through her, but she didn't own the power.

Jarod shared it with her. "Wine?"

"No thank you. I haven't had enough sleep to be able to hold my liquor tonight, and I think I very much want to be awake to see what happens next."

He nodded slowly. "We'll save it for later."

"If you like." She smiled. She couldn't help it. He brushed his calf against hers, and first date goose bumps rippled over her. God help her, she was twenty-nine, not nineteen.

He opened the water bottles and poured out drinks for each of them. Removing the plate toppers, he revealed a smorgasbord of skewers with steak, chicken, shrimp, and veggies. She laughed. "Appetizers?"

"Yep. I don't want to be too full for the main course." Any other man would have made it sound like a line, but his gaze swept over her in a raw caress. Her sex dampened, and she curled her toes into the carpeting as though trying to keep her ass planted on the chair— but why the hell was he sitting all the way over there?

He stroked her calf again. A light brush of his leg on hers and the caress ran a riot of sensation up her leg until her sex clenched tighter, as she imagined what it would be like to tangle their legs together, his body driving into hers.

"Kit Kat." His whisper teased her ears. Her eyes were closed, and she let out a shaky breath when forcing them open to stare at him.

"Yes?" It was the best she could do. She wanted to devour him. Dark, mysterious, sexy, dangerous, and thoughtful—he was all those things. She wanted to explore his body, snuggle up to it, sample it and hold him.

"Appetizers are meant to tease the palate."

She didn't know which one of them stood first, but she almost fell in her unsteady haste to stand. He caught her, easily sweeping her into an open-mouthed kiss which ended with them landing on the bed in a reckless tangle of arms and legs. His hands seemed to be everywhere, cupping a breast, pinching a nipple, delving between her thighs, and when he pressed his thumb to her clit, the world erupted in pleasure. She convulsed with the orgasm, clinging to him and riding his hand with fevered abandon.

He caressed her through the first orgasm and laved a wet, sucking kiss to one nipple before trailing another damp kiss over to the other. She bucked against his hand, the sweet tension snapping and throwing her over again as a second orgasm shook her. She'd rarely experienced two in one night, much less two so close together. He rolled away, and she let out a little whimper, but he murmured something.

Foil tore and he returned, covering her body with his and taking her mouth in another hot, wet invasion. His tongue tangled with hers as he seemed intent on devouring her. She surrendered to the passion, desperate to taste him. He slid his hands down to her thighs and urged one up, angling her leg, and then his cock glided against her clit, wrenching another wave of pleasure. She barely had time to grasp it before he slid into her sex and thrust to the hilt.

Her muscles took a moment to adjust, but she clung to him, staring up into his desire-laden eyes, and her heart squeezed at the want in them—the want and the tenderness. He held himself still, letting her get used to him. But she didn't want to wait. The delicious ache of being so full increased the pressure and pleasure tangling inside. She wrapped her legs around his hips, giving him freedom to thrust.

Every stroke of his cock driving home thrashed her with need, and she dug her nails into his back, arching her hips to meet him. They dangled on the precipice, every glide of his skin scorching her, each kiss digging deeper into her soul until he pushed her over the edge and his mouth claimed her scream as he followed her.

He collapsed and rolled to his back, draping her atop him as they panted. Their legs tangled, and her heart soared as the reality echoed her earlier imagining. She tucked her head against his chest, listening to the mad thrum-thrum of his heart. His fingers tangled in her hair, stroking her scalp lightly. He didn't let her go, a possessive arm locked around her waist, he kept her fastened to him.

She didn't want to go anywhere. The scent of their passion

perfumed the air around them, and she felt dizzy from wanting and having him all in the same embrace. She didn't want to move.

Ever.

"Jarod...."

"The time for second thoughts is long past, Kit Kat." His voice roughened, sleepy and more than a little arrogant. Arrogance he fully deserved.

"No second thoughts." She shifted to rest her chin on his chest and gaze up at him. He still panted, and tremors raced through his body. A sense of power flooded her—she made him feel so much.

"Good."

"But...."

He groaned and pinched her bottom. "Yes, I love your ass."

Laughing, she nibbled a bite of his skin—hot, salty, and completely masculine. Her sex clenched around his softening cock, and he hissed out another breath. "Thank you, but I was trying to say thank you."

Lifting his head, he gazed at her, the stern expression completely gone, replaced with a naked tenderness which snapped shackles around her heart. "For what?"

"For trusting me."

He tugged her up and their mouths collided in a sweeter kiss, soaked in passion. They clung to each other, exploring, teasing, and adoring. She sighed. He owned a piece of her whether he realized it or not. Her secret agent man had infiltrated her heart and set up shop when she hadn't paid attention. A tear splashed down her cheek, and Jarod pulled back to look at her.

"Hey...." Concern darkened his voice.

"I want to—no—I want and I need to tell you the truth, now."

He stroked her hair back from her forehead. "You don't have to."

"I know." She did. She recognized baring the soul wasn't for everyone. "Keeping it from you—it wasn't about protecting me or holding myself back, but now it feels like it is, and I don't want lies between us."

Blowing out a slow breath, he nodded, and, with one arm against the bed, he shifted them both up until he rested against the pillows and she snuggled against him. "You haven't lied to me, Kit Kat."

"No, but I haven't been completely honest, either."

"Arguably, neither have I." His swift agreement and aligning himself on her side bolstered her confidence. He'd not lied to her either. They'd omitted a lot, but they'd fought for truth in every stage of the game.

She opened her mouth, but he pressed a finger against her lips and stared at her steadily. "Whatever you tell me, whatever 'truth' you reveal, changes nothing between us."

Pondering his words, she shook her head. "Truth always changes things."

"No, truth only changes the illusion. I know you, and I don't have any illusions. You have a life and a past, and you've made choices. But you're not flippant or reckless or entitled, no matter your upbringing. So I know the truth of you, Kit Kat. Tell me what you feel the need to, but you don't have to."

The anxiety twisting her stomach settled, and she nodded slowly. "The same goes for you, you know?"

A wry grin curved his lips. "My life is a lot darker than yours, Kit Kat, and there are things I can't tell you."

"National security." It wasn't a guess.

He said nothing, but massaged her back in gentle, circular strokes.

"Okay." She accepted his silence as the answer. "I won't put you in the position of having to explain."

His expression softened, and she laughed, shifting to wipe the traces of damp tears from her face. "You realize this is a completely odd conversation."

"I've had stranger," he teased. "But not with anyone as lovely or as interesting."

"Good." She exhaled. The time for putting off the truth was over. "I told you about my mother...." She waited for his nod before continuing. "When I went looking for her, I also found my grandfather—her father—a man named Sebastian Kant. He was a thief."

Chapter Ten

L ocated on about fifteen acres, the hospice offered a park-like setting for both recuperating patients and those soon bidding farewell to the world. The serenity of the location, coupled with the competent staff and the latest technology, offered the best possible care, and they'd done everything she asked for the cantankerous old man she adored. Several of the staff recognized her when she walked in, tote bag in hand. They gave her quiet smiles of welcome, friendly nods—each served up with a dose of sympathy.

Sebastian was not long for this world, a fact she'd had more than a year to accept, and yet grief still clawed at her throat. She walked down the long corridor toward the private suite ensuring him his dignity and comfort. The medical reports said he rarely roused from his bed most days and his brightest moments came when she called.

Regret flickered like a candle guttering in a hard breeze. She could have spent the last year with him, save for the wretched phone call so many months before when he confessed to sending someone out to steal *The Fortunate Buddha*. She didn't think she'd understood him and cut short a ski trip and business negotiation to fly halfway around the world. His mind wandered sometimes—congestive heart failure depriving his brain of critical oxygen and blood supply. They were fortunate he didn't have more strokes.

At the door to his room, she paused to collect herself. Farther down the hallway, the door to the stairwell swung closed, but she didn't see anyone.

"Go see your grandfather and don't worry about anything. You'll have your time with him." Jarod's promise echoed in her ears.

She ignored the closing door, exhaled a long breath to release the anxiety, and let herself into Sebastian Kant's room.

Machines beeped in quiet testimony to his heart's continued efforts. The big man lay against the sheets, nearly as pale as the blankets covering him. His weathered face, once tanned and filled with laughter, was solemn in sleep. Wrinkles fanned out in deep grooves from the corners of his eyes. The old man lying there bore only a passing resemblance to the vital man she'd gotten to know and adore over the years. The shopping bag's weight cut into her hand.

"Grandpa?" She pitched her voice low, unwilling to disturb him if his rest was deeper than a doze.

He blinked, revealing a pair of pale-green eyes—they'd been a deeper color once upon a time. The first time they met, she'd seen her own eyes reflected back at her. Neither of her parents had green eyes, so she'd never understood the visceral connection to another the way she did to her grandfather.

Until Jarod.

"Hello, baby girl." He wheezed the words and punctuated them with a cough.

Brushing her lips against his cool, dry cheek, she forced the tears burning behind her eyes to stay there. "How are you?" She perched on the edge of the bed and set the bag on the floor near her feet.

"Better now you're here. Missed you."

"Missed you, too. I'm sorry it took me so long to get back. I've been trying for a while." Morocco. Geneva. New York. A long while. She sniffed, swallowing the mourning ache and keeping her expression warm and teasing. "But I knew you'd wait for me."

"As long as I can." In his prime, Sebastian Kant had been a handsome, dapper man. A con man from a young age, he used his charm to woo wealthy women and men alike. The women all fell a little bit in love with him, and the men wanted to be his friends or partners. He took his act from small time to large with a series of jewel heists that earned him notice and prestige. His best friends were also his thief buddies, and the stories he used to tell would make her sides burn with laughter. Quite the rogue, he took on more and complex jobs, acquiring priceless artifacts and gems from around the globe.

"The doctors told me you haven't been eating and they want to give you a feeding tube." The utter indignity of the last call had come before her meeting in New York. The doctor insisted Sebastian wasn't in his right mind anymore and his refusal to eat was tantamount to suicide.

"You told them no?" Wandering and exhausted as the old man might be, he fixed her with a sharp look.

"Of course I did. I made you a promise, and I'll keep it. But you do need to try and eat," she chided him.

Sebastian didn't want to be kept alive by machine. The vitality of the man seeped away with every passing month, but his pride remained intact. His only regret—or at least the only one he ever expressed to her—was the failure ending his lucrative career all those years before. The failure landed his best friends long prison sentences—in a foreign country.

They both died in Thailand, leaving Sebastian to mourn them with a laurel of guilt and responsibility he wore to this day.

"Louis called. The boy is in town and promised to come see me." He coughed again. She'd expected as much. Sebastian had mentored Louis when the viscount was at university and while her relationship with Louis was adversarial at best, Sebastian still saw him as a rebellious young man and not the psychopath he'd grown up to be. "He tried to get the Buddha for me. I gave him the plans. But the partners he brought into the deal...they stole it." Sebastian sighed. "I almost had it once, did I tell you?"

A thump in the hallway pulled her attention, but the door didn't move, and she saw no one in the rectangular observation window. "Yes, sir. I remember."

"Pete, Jim, and I—we were riding high on the best summer of our lives. We'd toured Europe, courtesy of the wealthy." Sebastian rambled now, his wheezing straining every third word. "But Pete heard about the temple and the Buddha, and he said to me, 'Sebastian, it's the score of a lifetime. They say if you rub his belly, you'll be blessed with good fortune for all your days. Think about what we could do if we had it.'"

She could recite the story with him, but she didn't interrupt, taking his almost papery, thin hand in hers and rubbing it between her palms. "So you found a way to take the train from Paris to India—an exotic journey to be certain."

He coughed and grinned. "Exactly so, and, from there, we hiked or borrowed cars until we reached the mountains. We were nearly out of funds by the time we got to Thailand, but we didn't care—it was a lark, an adventure, a wild ride." Then his smile faded. "We found the temple, studied it, knew when the monks prayed and when they were out in their gardens. We knew the security layout, the location, and we were ready."

It didn't matter how well she knew the tale. Her heart always began to hammer when it came to this part. Another impact—this time a clang—punched through the sound barrier of the door. She glanced back but found the door to his room remained shut.

"It was late and dark. The monks' final prayers were done. We climbed up the rocky slope, scaling it like three drunk fools, without rope. We could handle it. Plenty of crevices and places for us to get handholds. It went fine, we made it into the temple, and there he was, all golden and waiting for us. I picked him up—he's smaller than you might expect—but the craftsmanship.... It's as though he winks at you." Sebastian coughed. "I was about to put him in my bag when the army showed up."

This part of the story blurred the lines between reality and guilt. "They flooded into the room like ants. I still had the Buddha in my hands. We raced to the wall overlooking the ravine. I'd barely slung a leg over when they grabbed Jim. He yelled for us to keep going, and Pete gave me a shove—but I dropped the Buddha—it wasn't quite in my bag—and then they had Pete. I let go of the wall and slid down the rocky outface, cutting my hands and arms, but I made it to the bottom and away. They didn't."

He sighed, coughing until she could get a cup and straw to his lips. He drank, but his watery gaze remained shrouded in sorrow. "If I hadn't dropped it, they would have gotten away. The luck would have held, and it was when everything went wrong."

"I know Grandpa." She set the cup down.

"And it's not for me I wanted Louis to fetch the Buddha. You know...we have to break the cycle. Your mama wouldn't have left you if it hadn't been for me."

She didn't have the heart to tell him her mother's addictions were not the fault of some Asian artifact. They'd argued this point before. Her grandfather believed it. Just as he believed by dropping the Buddha, he'd broken his lucky streak and sentenced his friends to die in prison far away from home. Losing the job broke something in him, something he'd never been able to repair.

"Grandpa...."

"This is important, Kitten. You have to get Louis to help you find whoever took the Buddha from him. I know he paid someone—I gave them all the instructions, the layout, everything. But the man ran off with it rather than give it to Louis." He tried to sit up, and she pressed a hand to his shoulder, but it was too late. He shook with the coughs racking his body.

"Grandpa, listen to me. You with me again?" She searched his face, and, when he nodded slowly, she helped him take another drink before picking the bag up off the floor. "Louis wasn't bringing the Buddha to you and never intended to. He was auctioning it to the highest bidder." Twice, she wanted to add, first to the French ambassador and then later, in Geneva, after he'd smuggled it home from Morocco. She'd intended to intercept it, but the diplomatic pouch he used cut short her plans.

"No. He promised, Kitten...."

Her chest squeezed in sympathy. "I know, but he lied. The viscount is a thief, Grandpa. A thief and a liar and a cheat. But it doesn't matter."

"It does. I wanted to fix it for you, fix your mama, and make sure when I finally kick off you aren't left with my bad luck."

She sighed. "Grandpa, that's what I'm trying to tell you. I—" She stopped trying to fumble the explanation and bent down to open the box inside the bag. Nestled carefully amongst the packing materials, the golden Buddha winked up at her. It was cool to the touch, the metal smooth, almost liquid satin in its softness. Made from pure gold, the monetary value of the Buddha was incalculable—but the wealth wasn't what her Grandfather wanted nor was it why she'd devoted so many man-hours in the last year to getting it back for him.

"I have something for you, Grandpa." She set it on the bed between them. Taking his hand, she wrapped his gnarled fingers around the Buddha's hip, his fingertips brushing its belly.

"It's—" He wheezed, pulling himself upright before she could stop him. He lifted the statue and stared at it, the exhaustion and grief in his face transforming to something rapturous. All the worry and anxiety in her gut washed away as he began to smile. "This is the Buddha, Kitten. You have to rub its belly."

"I'm fine, Grandpa. You rub his belly." She'd held the Buddha a half-dozen times this year. Each time it weighed more heavily on her soul. She wanted to grant him this last wish and then she would take it home. Correction, she and Jarod would take it home.

"I'm sorry," Sebastian whispered, but he wasn't talking to her. His gaze remained fixed on the Buddha in his hand. "I'm really sorry I tried to take you, and I left you all behind. Please forgive my family and make it better for them."

Tears gathered in her eyes, and she fought a losing effort to keep them from escaping. Sebastian leaned back against the pillows, cradling the Buddha like a baby. "It will be okay for you now, Kitten—" He wheezed a long, raspy breath at the end of the word and stopped.

Kit jerked up and looked at the machines, which screamed an alarm. Swinging her gaze back, she found Sebastian's eyes were closed and his face relaxed. "No. Come on, Grandpa. No...."

The door flung open, and a pair of nurses came in. They ushered her back from the bed. One nurse plucked the statue out of her grandfather's hands and passed it to her. She took it, holding it loosely as she watched in numbed shock. Sebastian Kant died with a smile on his face, the ache of more than fifty years of grief eased from his expression.

After ten minutes, a doctor walked in and called it. He murmured apologies; so did the nurses. They talked to her, but she didn't hear them. She could only see her grandfather's beatific expression and hear the quiet joy in his voice. She'd lost the last year of his life to this Don Quixote quest, but she couldn't deny him the last chance to right what he felt went so horribly wrong.

The Buddha warmed under her touch, but the rest of the room faded. The voices of the doctor and the nurses drifted past her from a great distance. She nodded when they paused, and shook their hands. All the arrangements for the funeral home were in his file. They would take care of everything. They finally left her alone, and she moved with wooden slowness to store the Buddha back in its box. If she never saw the damn thing again, it would be too soon.

His cheek was cool when she bent to press a last kiss to it. "Good-bye, Grandpa. I hope, wherever you are, you're happy again." A hot tear escaped, and she swiped at it. She wanted to stay here and hold his hand, but he was gone, and what good would it do him anymore? Straightening, she picked up the bag and tried to memorize the peace in his expression. She wanted to hold onto the last memory—for both of them.

Leaving his room, she walked up the hallway, blinded by her

tears. More nurses came out. One patted her arm, another rubbed her shoulder, and a third—a stout woman who'd attended her grandfather from his admission to the hospice eighteen months before—gave her a hug. Kit murmured some appropriate words to each, accepting their condolences before moving on to the next wave. The sunshine blinded her as she walked outside, but she didn't reach for her sunglasses.

It took every ounce of her willpower to put one foot in front of the other. She was almost to the car when a man stepped into her path. She looked up to see a stranger, his hand outstretched to take the bag in her hand. She stared at him numbly, but he never touched her or the bag. Jarod's arm snaked around the assailant's neck, and the man grunted and slowly went to the ground, unconscious.

Jarod tugged the man behind a line of bushes and came back to her. "Kit Kat?"

She sighed and burrowed into his arms, giving him the bag and letting her tears fall.

"Jarod, Louis duMonde knows my grandfather. Grandpa...Grandpa blamed himself for a heist gone wrong a long time ago. He'd known duMonde since his teen years, and he used to mentor him. When he was diagnosed with congestive heart failure, he called duMonde and told him how to get the Buddha. He has to know where I am going." Kit told him the whole story, including her involvement after duMonde failed to deliver the item as promised. After tracing the artifact, she'd followed Louis and the item from Morocco to Geneva. Later, she found the information on Anya in his safe and left it for her, taking only the statue. It only took pulling a few strings to get the Buddha into the States using a museum, but, like her, Louis's training came from her grandfather. He'd anticipated the move.

He'd turned a curator at the museum and sent his men to claim the piece before she could. It was when Kit used her friendship with Pietr to befriend Sophie and cultivate her own connection. When the Buddha ended up in police evidence, she charmed her way in and sent it out via the internal post system. Packages entering a police station were scanned—not those leaving.

All she wanted was to grant a dying man his last request. If Louis knew about the hospice, he didn't doubt the Frenchman would have men waiting for her. He'd sent her in—scouting ahead first to deal with the two men in the lobby. She'd picked up a tail on her drive in, and he'd dealt with those men while she bid her grandfather good-bye.

Another pair were sleeping off a cocktail of sedatives in the stairwell.

The seventh, and final, now lay under a bush. Jarod sent a text to an asset and let the man get the Bakersfield police to pick these men up. He ushered Kit back into the car and stowed the bag in the backseat. When she fell silent, he let her cry and held her hand when her tears turned to hiccups and finally to empty despair.

The loss of a parent or a grandparent was not an easy burden. She'd focused so much of her energy on giving the old one man his last wish she'd hidden from the grief of losing him. He kept a wary eye on the rearview mirror, but no one followed them. As for duMonde, he was on a plane, confident his men would snatch the Buddha back for him. The bastard had likely already arranged an alibi.

"In the early 1970s, the Cold War was in full force, and agencies on both sides of the pond worked to outsmart the other." He turned onto the freeway and headed for the airport and her private plane. She would come back for the funeral, but, for now, he wanted her off the ground in Los Angeles and away from any other messengers Louis might send until he dealt with the viscount. "My father was an up-and-coming analyst. He discovered a group of foreign agents communicating via rare book auctions. They would hide the messages on the blank pages in invisible ink—one agent would put it up for auction and another would purchase it. He intercepted more than a dozen before he broke the code."

She sniffled and let go of his hand to claim some tissues from her bag. "What did he do with them?" There she was. Beneath the layers of sadness and regret, his Kit Kat began to rouse.

"He turned a report into his superiors, but they didn't see how they could use it to their advantage. My father suggested swapping one set of coded books out, intercepting them and replacing them with the dummy information."

"They could control the information flow and learn where they had leaks." She dabbed at her eyes.

"Exactly. He got a job at a rare book dealer and used the cover to handle the intercepts. He also got to know one of the agents who bought many of the books—a literature professor at a local university. When she came to auction, he always replaced whatever book she purchased with one of the coded ones he created...and one day, she brought in a coded one of her own to auction." Jarod smiled. Even amidst all the moves and countermoves, his father took the time to engage in a whimsical courtship. "He took the book she'd put up for auction, replaced it with another, tagged it with an isotope so they could track it. Later, he translated her book."

"I'm going to assume the message was important."

"It was. You see, in all the books she'd purchased, he'd included a second coded message. The first time, it was an introduction of sorts—a compliment to her beauty. Later, they were notes about the classes she taught and her interest in Renaissance writing. He knew everything about her—because he studied her—and he fell in love." He glanced sideways at her. Kit's mouth opened, but no words came out. "Now, remember, it's the cold war and consorting between agents happened but were also grounds for treason. He was very circumspect in his letters, never revealing his identity."

"And the one she sent back?" She latched onto the single, critical fact.

"A thank you for all his kind thoughts, but because of her work and her conflicted commitments, she didn't have much to offer." It was an opening, an access point his father could leverage. "He waited a week and set up another book drop. This time, he didn't wait for her superior's orders to come in, he'd already figured out most of the system. When she bought the book, she received the information he'd like to help her with the conflict. He could fix it for her...but she had to trust him."

Engaged in the story, Kit leaned forward and stared at him. "And?"

"And he walked into the director's office and pitched to him the benefits of turning a foreign agent and helping her defect. He cited all of her skills and qualifications and the fact that in every book he'd intercepted from her over the last year, she left out key data her superiors would have wanted—data she had to have access to."

"She was sabotaging her own mission."

"More or less." Jarod nodded. "At first, the director was reluctant. He required three tests of loyalty."

"And she passed them." Kit sniffled, but her confidence didn't waver.

"Yes, she did, but the director decided it would be better to turn her and send her back. That way she could provide information to the agency. My father disliked the idea, and when the director wouldn't change his mind, he warned the other agent as long as her cover remained intact—and she could safely return—they were going to ask her to."

She sucked in a little breath, and her fingers tightened against his. "What did she do?"

"She sent a blatant lie in her next coded message home. My father replaced it then took the evidence to the director. He told him the agent would rather die than go back, so she'd begun to dig her own grave. If they wanted to take advantage of her skill set, they needed to take her out of play."

"And they did?"

Jarod laughed softly at the impatience creeping into her voice. "Yes, it took a few more such messages and threats on both sides, but, eventually, the director caved. My father sold her a book with a single message in it—a date and location." He lifted Kit's hand and kissed a knuckle lightly.

"And?" She tugged her hand away and pinched him. Sadness still lingered in her gaze, but she sounded more like herself.

"And, he met her for dinner at a little French bistro in Washington D.C. By the end of their meal, he'd asked her to marry him and she said yes. An hour before she walked into the agency to turn herself in, they signed their marriage license."

"Oooh," Kit breathed. "She's your mother?"

"Yes, she is." Delighted at how swiftly she'd caught on, he grinned at her. "The director was furious, and they demoted Dad. He nearly got tossed out entirely, but they both knew the game, and they knew how to make it work. But what my mother and the director never understood was, from the moment he had her file, Dad fell in love with her. He knew he was going to get her out, and he'd only needed the time and the leverage to do it."

"That's so romantic."

He laughed again. "That's what my mom says."

"Doesn't your father think it's romantic?" she demanded, her red-rimmed eyes sparkling.

"No. He considers it a success." He claimed her hand for another kiss.

She laughed and leaned over to press a kiss to his cheek. "It's still romantic."

"I'm sure it is. You can argue the point with him when you meet them." He gauged her reaction from the corner of his eye.

Her sweet mouth curved into a delighted smile. "You want to introduce me to your parents?"

"I do."

She was silent long enough to give him pause, and then she gave him a smug look. "You know that's worth a point, right?"

He sighed. "Yes, darling. It's worth a point. Eight-six, it is."

"Eight?" she protested. "When did it become eight?"

One week later...

The Viscount duMonde glared at the news on his digital tablet. The return of *The Fortunate Buddha* to the temple in Thailand made the wires. The artifact's history and its recent ties to a pair of murders in New York were listed in the sidebar. He flexed his right hand; the bruise from his encounter at their airport still made his fingers twitch. He picked up the wine glass with his left and drained the contents. His waiter strolled over the moment he finished and set down a fresh glass, clearing away the empty.

"Is there anything else I can get you, sir?" The man's practiced tone edged on the patronizing, but his helpful expression settled Louis' ire. He shook his head and waved the man away. He would spend his afternoon getting drunk. The men he'd left to fetch the Buddha sat in a jail in Bakersfield, California, and two were threatening to roll over on him. It would cost, but they would be silenced.

Lady Hardwicke was in London. She'd flown home after the funeral—and a stop in Thailand, apparently. His stomach churned, and a burning sensation crept up through his chest. He took another swallow of the wine. His ulcer seemed to be acting up. He'd gained nothing from going after her, but teaching her to stay out of his business was a lesson she needed to learn. A cough surprised him, and he covered his mouth with a cloth napkin.

Another swig of wine and a second round of coughing as the burn in his stomach turned into a fire in his chest. He stared at the napkin as he lowered it.

Blood covered the cloth.

A fist wrapped around his heart and squeezed. He coughed

again and pitched out of the chair, pulling the table with him. Shouts came from the waitstaff, but the noise faded as the pain in his chest became unbearable and the light winked out.

Jarod wrapped the white coat around the bottle of wine and tucked both into a backpack. He slid his arms through the straps and knelt to tie his sneaker. A mixed playlist of symphony and hard rock played via his earbuds while he strolled to the bike rack to get the twelve-speed he'd locked up before entering the restaurant. The Paris streets hummed with activity in the midafternoon.

The phone in his pocket vibrated, and he tugged it out and scanned the text message. After a week with his parents and a couple of side trips, he'd sent Kit home to London while he paused to deal with duMonde. He had left a book in her bag—a racy historical which had caught her eye at the airport—with a message in it. He knew she'd ferret out the story from his parents, and his mother had showed her exactly how to read hidden messages.

So, he left a proposal for her in code.

The text was her answer.

Yes.

He laughed when the phone buzzed with a second text message.

Ten-eleven, my point. Did you seriously think I wouldn't find the ring in my own jewelry box?

He sent back *Twelve-eleven—it's only the engagement ring.*

Dad was right—this was how one defined success.

About the Author

National bestselling author, Heather Long, likes long walks in the park, science fiction, superheroes, Marines, and men who aren't douche bags. Her books are filled with heroes and heroines tangled in romance as hot as Texas summertime. From paranormal historical westerns to contemporary military romance, Heather might switch genres, but one thing is true in all of her stories--her characters drive the books. When she's not wrangling her menagerie of animals, she devotes her time to family and friends she considers family. She believes if you like your heroes so real you could lick the grit off their chest, and your heroines so likable, you're sure you've been friends with women just like them, you'll enjoy her worlds as much as she does.

Also by Heather Long

Always a Marine
Series so Far (in order by release)

Once Her Man, Always Her Man
Luke & Rebecca

Retreat Hell! She Just Got Here
Logan, Jazz & Zach

Tell It to the Marine
James & Lauren
Introduction of Matt McCall and Damon Sinclair
Features an appearance of Logan Cavanaugh

Proud to Serve Her
Damon & Helena
Matt, James, Lauren, Luke and Rebecca mentioned

Her Marine
Brody & Shannon

No Regrets, No Surrender
Logan, Jazz & Zach
James featured

The Marine Cowboy
A.J. & Sheri
Phone call from Luke

The Two and the Proud
Rowdy & Kim

A Marine and a Gentleman
Brenden & Liam
Appearances of James, Logan, Jazz, Shannon, Rebecca, Lauren

Combat Barbie
Kyle & Mary
Jazz makes an appearance via phone

Whiskey Tango Foxtrot
Joe & Melody
James makes an appearance

What Part of Marine Don't You Understand?
Matt & Naomi
Appearances by James and Logan, Damon is mentioned

A Marine Affair
Eli & Rick

Marine Ever After
Paul & Lillianna
Multiple appearances at Luke & Rebecca's wedding

Marine in the Wind
Greg & Georgia
Appearances by A.J. & Sheri

Marine with Benefits
Derek & Kara
Appearance by Logan

A Marine of Plenty
Charlie & Jana
Appearance by Naomi

A Candle for a Marine
Isaac & Zehava
Appearances by Zach & Shannon

Marine Under the Mistletoe
Kaiden & Rowan

Have Yourself a Marine Christmas
Rebel & Noel
Appearances by Derek, Kara, Luke and James

Lest Old Marines Be Forgot
Tom & Brenda
Appearances by Luke, James, Logan, and Damon

Her Marine Bodyguard
Shannon & Brody
Multiple appearances including Luke, Logan, Zach, Jazz, Mary,
Damon & Rowdy

ROAR Series
Mischief, Mongrels & Mayhem

The Black Hills Wolves
What a Wolf Wants
Wolf in Winter Clothing
Scent of Madness

The Love Thieves
Catch Me
Treasure Me
Hunt Me

www.ingramcontent.com/pod-product-compliance
Lightning Source LLC
Chambersburg PA
CBHW070342130626
46556CB00007B/2994